The Duke's Loveless Bargain

HISTORICAL REGENCY ROMANCE NOVEL

Dorothy Sheldon

Copyright © 2025 by Dorothy Sheldon
All Rights Reserved.
This book may not be reproduced or transmitted in any form without the written permission of the publisher. In no way is it legal to reproduce, duplicate, or transmit any part of this document in either electronic means or in printed format. Recording of this publication is strictly prohibited and any storage of this document is not allowed unless with written permission from the publisher.

Table of Contents

Prologue 4
Chapter One 11
Chapter Two 18
Chapter Three 25
Chapter Four 32
Chapter Five 38
Chapter Six 42
Chapter Seven 47
Chapter Eight 51
Chapter Nine 57
Chapter Ten 64
Chapter Eleven 71
Chapter Twelve 78
Chapter Thirteen 85
Chapter Fourteen 92
Chapter Fifteen 98
Chapter Sixteen 106
Chapter Seventeen 114
Chapter Eighteen 121
Chapter Nineteen 128

Chapter Twenty 135
Chapter Twenty-One 142
Chapter Twenty-Two 150
Epilogue 157

Prologue

Stonehaven Manor, Sixteen Years Previously

"Look at the board, boy, look at the board. What does it *say*?"

That tapping noise, which was the sound of a long, thin switch against the blackboard, was starting to appear in Jasper's dreams. He'd dreamt about it just last night, along with Mr. Fyre's thin, cadaverous face, with those awful bulging pale eyes.

"Look at the board, boy!" the schoolmaster repeated, tapping the switch again. Swallowing hard, Jasper forced himself to stare at the blackboard.

The board was full of markings, shapes and lines which he knew were meant to represent words. Other boys his own age could interpret them with ease, he knew that from his humiliatingly brief time at Eton. In moments of desperation, he had asked a few of them how they learned so easily, but they only stared at him, blinking in confusion, and replied that they just *did*.

Mr. Fyre took a step towards him, and Jasper flinched.

The schoolroom was icy cold. Mr. Fyre said that it helped to "cool" the mind, whatever that meant, and since winter was well along, there was a thin film of ice on the inside of the windowpanes. Jasper's hands were numb with cold, the nail beds faintly mauve, which had done nothing to improve his efforts at writing on his slate.

He curled his fingers into fists and forced himself to stay still as the schoolmaster stalked towards, whipping the switch to and fro in front of him.

"There is a single sentence written on that blackboard, sirrah," Mr. Fyre said, his voice deceptively cool and calm. "You will do me the honour of reading it aloud. At once."

Jasper swallowed dryly. What time was it? It seemed like an age since breakfast, but he was terrified of glancing at the clock behind him and learning that it was barely ten o' clock. Schooldays dragged, painfully so. The palms of his hands still smarted from yesterday's lessons.

He stared at the blackboard, fear tasting acrid in his mouth, and willed the letters to make sense. The first word he could just about recognize – it was his name, with the characteristic J at the start, and a swooping P halfway through. The next two words were short, only three letters between them.

Perhaps it would be easier if Mr. Fyre's handwriting was a little simpler, something bold and easy to decipher, like the print in a book. Instead, the man insisted on curling, looping words that even experienced readers struggled to decipher. Or so Janey said, and *she* could read and write just fine, even if she *was* only the head housemaid.

"J-Jasper," he began, gasping a little, "Jasper i-is a... a... st.... sta..." he stammered and stuttered, the longer fourth word refusing to make sense at all. The more he squinted, the more the letters jumbled themselves up. He swallowed hard, aware of Mr. Fyre prowling closer and closer. Jasper stuttered for a few minutes, and then eventually fell silent.

The words weren't going to come. They never did when he was frightened or under pressure. Mr. Fyre was behind him now, circling him slowly like a predator rounding its prey.

"Very disappointing, sirrah, very disappointing indeed," he murmured, voice low. If Jasper hadn't known better, he might have thought that the man *was* disappointed, truly.

Fortunately, Jasper *did* know better. He clenched his fists tighter and tighter, staring ahead at the blackboard until the words blurred, becoming even more unintelligible.

With a sigh that might have sounded as if he *almost* regretted what must be done, Mr. Fyre came to stand at Jasper's side, testing the strength of the switch. He glanced past Jasper, to the shadowy corner behind them both.

"You see, Your Grace? I do my best, but the boy simply does not want to learn. However, I shall persist. Hold out your hands, sirrah."

Jasper numbly held out his hands, palms up, in a practised motion. His skin was already stinging in anticipation. Mr. Fyre lifted the switch.

"Wait a moment, Mr. Fyre," came a deep voice from the corner. The schoolmaster was already bringing the switch down, and nearly lost his balance in an effort to halt his own momentum.

Taken aback, he glanced over at the third occupant of the room.

"Your Grace? Discipline is vital in these matters, especially when..."

A tall, broad-shouldered man came stepping forward, his black hair flecked with premature grey. He yawned, looking bored.

"I will handle this, Mr. Fyre. Go to the kitchen and request a cup of tea. I'll summon you back when lessons can resume."

"But, Your Grace..."

"I said," the Duke of Stonehaven responded, ice creeping into his voice, "that I would handle it. I am not used to repeating myself."

Mr. Fyre quailed at that. Mumbling something and dropping his gaze, he hurried for the door, stopping only to set the switch down across Jasper's desk.

The door closed, and a heavy silence descended on the room. Jasper let his hands drop to his side, and fixed his gaze on the blackboard.

"You truly can't read it, then," the Duke said, voice clipped.

"No, Father. I cannot. I... I have tried, truly."

"There is no such thing as *trying* in this world, my boy. One either does a thing, or one does not. That is all that matters."

The Duke heaved a sigh, raking a hand through his hair. Jasper bit his lip and tried to stand as still as possible.

"I'm sure you cannot believe it, but I was remarkably pleased when you were born," the Duke said suddenly. "A baby within the first year of marriage, a *son*. I was thrilled. Little did I know that there would be no more children, not even daughters, and that my *son* would turn out to be little more than simple-minded. My son would, at the age of twelve, be unable to *read*!"

On the last word, he brought his fist down onto the desk in front of Jasper with a resounding *crash*. It echoed around the room, and Jasper fought not to flinch.

It is not fair. I am trying. I am trying. It's not my fault the words jump about. They don't make sense.

"I am not simple-minded," he said. To his horror, he spoke aloud.

The Duke turned his head slowly to look down at his son.

"I beg your pardon?"

Sucking in a breath, Jasper forced himself to look up. His father did not like to be looked in the eye, everybody knew that, but he couldn't seem to stop himself. They had the same eyes, everybody said so. A clear blue – true blue, not tinted by grey or gold or even green, but a pure, sky-blue – fringed with black lashes and framed by heavy black brows.

As far as Jasper could tell, their eyes were the only similarities he and his father shared. He was entirely happy for it to remain that way.

"I am not simple-minded, Father," Jasper forced himself to say. "I am not. I can't... can't read and write very well, and I don't understand why not, but I am not simple-minded."

The Duke only stared at him, unblinking.

"Then read out the sentence on the blackboard."

Jasper's eyes blurred with tears. He fought not to let them fall – crying only made the Duke a hundred times more angry.

"I can't."

"Shall I read it to you?" the Duke said, although it was not really a question. He turned to look at the board, and read out, with perfect diction: "Jasper is a simple-minded fool, but may yet excel with careful tutelage and discipline. There. That is what it says."

He could have chosen an easier sentence for me to read, Jasper thought sourly. He said nothing, of course.

The Duke stood in front of him, arms folded behind his back, head cocked.

"I do not know what to do with you, Jasper. I even heard a rumour that some brainless housemaid was meddling in your teaching, which might explain why Mr. Fyre's methods are not working as well as they should."

"Nobody else is teaching me, Father," Jasper lied at once. Janey would be dismissed, no doubt, if their secret lessons were revealed. People could be cruel, like the parents at Eton who had called Mr. Pippin a milk-and-water-master, whatever that meant, even though his careful, gentle methods were the only thing that had seemed to help Jasper learn at all.

Mr. Pippin was gone, of course, and no amount of begging could convince the Duke to hire *him* as a private tutor, instead of Mr. Fyre.

The Duke stared down at his only son, anger and disappointment fizzling in his eyes. Jasper forced himself to look.

"Well, we must persist," the Duke said at last. "Mr. Fyre is a good teacher, and an excellent disciplinarian. I have no doubt that your inability to learn stems from your own obstinacy. I am confident that you shall endeavour to improve in the future. Now, extend your hands."

Jasper held out his hands again, palms up, and his father picked up the switch.

***

His palms throbbed and stung, but at least he had been granted the rest of the day off. It wasn't out of kindness, but because his palms and fingers were now too swollen and raw to hold a piece of chalk.

Jasper hurried along the endless, dark hallways that criss-crossed Stonehaven Manor.

When I'm grown up, he thought for the thousandth time, *I'm going to leave this place forever.*

He wasn't a fool. His father would not live forever, and when he died, Jasper would become the Duke of Stonehaven. And then his life would change.

I will dismiss that awful Mrs. Price, he thought gleefully, *and have Janey Nettle as housekeeper instead. Everybody likes her, and she's kind and clever. I shall have Mr. Pippin come here* to instruct me in the art of reading – I am certain I would make good progress under his tutelage – and all shall be well.

He rounded a corner and found himself in the largest parlour in the house, face to face with his parents' portrait hanging ten feet high. It was a stark reminder that he was *not* the duke, and was not, in fact, anyone important at all.

The Blue Parlour, as it was called, was near the front of the house and was generally used to receive guests. Privately, Jasper hated how each room had to have a specific purpose. Why couldn't rooms just be rooms? Some of the tenants on their land only had a handful of rooms in their entire home, perhaps even one or two!

A shape stirred on the chaise longue, underneath the tall, glaring portraits.

"Jasper, darling? What are you doing out of the schoolroom? You may come here and kiss me, if you like."

Jasper went forward obediently to kiss his mother.

The Duchess had always been a thin woman, pale and delicate, as the fashion required. Her portrait was white-skinned and elegant, large dark eyes peering out of a beautiful, dainty face. In recent years, her thinness had turned to something almost skeletal, the sort of frame that made doctors glance meaningfully at each other and whisper in corners.

Jasper knew that his father raged at his mother, infuriated at her refusal to either die – and therefore allow him to marry again – or produce another child. These days, she seemed closer to dying than producing a sibling for Jasper, and yet she held on.

He kissed her cold, papery cheek, and she smiled tiredly up at him.

"You look very much like your papa, Jasper. Now, go on and finish your lessons."

"I have no lessons today, Mama. Mr. Fyre said so."

"Oh?" the Duchess yawned, disinterested. "Then go and play."

"I want to talk to you, Mama."

She shifted, turning her head away from him. "I am too tired for that, my dear. Go and play."

He didn't move. "Mama, do you think I am simple-minded?"

She opened her eyes a little wider. "Who said that you were simple-minded?"

"Papa."

"Oh," the Duchess rested a little heavier against her pillows. "Well, I hate to say it, but your papa is generally right about things."

Jasper's cheeks burned. "I am *not* simple-minded, Mama! I was very good at many subjects at Eton. I could do mathematics much easier than the other boys, and geometry. Not Latin, but I could remember all sorts of things, if somebody would read it out to me. Once, I..."

The Duchess waved a languid hand. "I am *very* tired, Jasper. Why don't you go and play? Or do some lessons with Mr. Fyre?"

He bit his lip. "I told you, Mama, I have no lessons today. I thought you might talk to Papa and tell him that I am not what he thinks I am. I thought you might help me."

The Duchess shifted to look at him again, and her dark eyes were blank and flat.

"If you do not want your papa to think of you as simple, Jasper, then you must learn to read and write. I am sure that if you apply yourself, you will find that it is not hard at all. Now, off you go, I am very tired."

Jasper hesitated, and some of his reluctance must have transferred itself to his mother. The Duchess opened her eyes wider again.

"Jasper, do not be stubborn. Already you have gotten poor Janey into a great deal of trouble, over those secret lessons you were having."

He sucked in a breath. "She... she was only trying to help, Mama. With my reading."

"What use does a maid have for reading?" the Duchess muttered, seeming peevish all of a sudden. "I liked Janey very much, but the housekeeper said that she was getting *above herself*, and so she has been removed from being head housemaid and sent back down into the kitchen. She is nine-and-twenty and thus it shall prove a most arduous undertaking for her to navigate such circumstances, with little prospect of advancement thereafter. That is your fault, Jasper."

His face burned. Tears pricked at his eyes, but Jasper bit his lower lip until the pain distracted him from crying. He could not cry. Men did not cry. *Dukes* did not cry, not even if their hands were switched until they could not close their fingers into fists. His father's words echoed in his head, taunting in their accuracy.

Nobody will help you in this world, my boy. Better keep your feelings to yourself and concentrate on not being left behind. If you shed another tear, a single tear more, I shall have to give you ten more strokes.

"That is not fair," Jasper heard himself say. "She didn't deserve that."

"We never get what we deserve in this world," the Duchess responded at once, closing her eyes. "I am very tired, Jasper. Go on back to the schoolroom and carry on with your lessons."

He swallowed, feeling bone-tired all of a sudden. "I have no more lessons today, Mama."

"Don't you? You should have told me so, then."

"I... I did tell you so."

"I am tired, Jasper," the Duchess repeated, feeling for a thin blanket tossed over her lower body, and hauling it up to her chin. "Go and play."

After a moment, it was clear that there would be no more conversation from his mother. He turned and tiptoed silently away, leaving the still, stale air of the Blue Parlour behind.

Nobody is going to help me, he thought suddenly, the idea landing in his head like a cannonball, stopping him in his tracks. *Mr. Fyre does not care about helping me. Father only cares about his reputation and that I am his only son. Mama... Mama never thinks about me at all, I think. Anybody who does want to help me – like Janey or Mr. Pippin – are only taken away from me.*

If I want to be helped, I shall have to help myself.

He squeezed his hands into fists, nearly crying out aloud at the pain. The pain was good, though, making him angry and staving off the sudden, ice-cold sadness the bloomed up inside and threatened to make him sick.

He had known, deep down, that nobody was ever going to help him, or understand – except perhaps poor, demoted Janey – but now, the knowledge had bloomed and taken root. It was no longer a feeling. It was a fact.

Jasper Demeridge, heir to the dukedom of Stonehaven, was entirely alone in the world, and would have to make his choices accordingly.

Chapter One

London, Sixteen Years Later

The ball was, as all good parties were in the height of the Season, a tremendous crush.

Unfortunately, that was literal. Holding her breath and lifting the two glasses of lemonade to shoulder height in an attempt to stop them spilling, Margaret wriggled through the last of the crowd and came out in a small circle of space near the wall.

There was a row of chairs circling the ballroom, designed for the infirm and for chaperones and matrons, but also for tired young ladies who had few acquaintances and few to no names on their dance cards.

Like Margaret, for instance.

Mr. Arthur Green was sitting where she had left him, spreading out his thin frame to keep all three seats free. He smiled nervously as she approached, lifting a hand to fiddle with his spectacles, like the shy young man that he was.

"Thank you, Miss Molyneaux, you are very kind. I really should have fetched the lemonade myself."

She smiled. "It's quite alright, Mr. Green."

Privately, she thought that the nervy, mild-mannered Mr. Green would have had worse luck in forcing his way through the crowd than she had. She handed over one lemonade, and glanced around, a frown furrowing her brow.

"Where is Marigold?"

"Hm? Oh, Miss Marigold is dancing, I think. A gentleman came to ask her shortly after you went for the lemonade."

Margaret bit back a sigh. Marigold was seventeen, and really too young to be *out* at all, but their mother had decided that this would be her year, and so here she was. She seemed to be exclusively targeted by leering old gentlemen, and almost all of Margaret's time was taken up with fending them off. She had no time to look for a suitor of her own, although Mr. Green *did* seem promising.

He was around twenty years old, two years younger than herself, the fourth or fifth brother in some rich household with not too many prospects for himself beyond what his own wits could carve out. So far, Margaret had found him difficult to talk to and almost comically afraid of most women, but he was kind, and one never knew where these things might go.

She peered around and caught sight of Marigold in the middle of the dance floor. Immediately, her heart dropped.

"It's a waltz," she said aloud. Mr. Green, mid-sip, spluttered.

"Why, I... yes, I suppose it is."

"Marigold isn't supposed to waltz."

Mr. Green shifted uneasily. "Oh. I did not know you were opposed to the waltz. I know that some people *do* find it rather improper, but..."

"I don't find it improper, not for a grown woman who can decide whether she wants to waltz or not, but my sister is barely seventeen, and she expressed discomfort with the dance. And is that... is that Lord Tumnus?"

She knew it was, even before she said the words. The wretched man was close to forty these days and had never so much as looked twice at a woman over the age of nineteen. In fact, his tastes were rumoured to run even younger than that, which perhaps explained why he had pounced on Marigold with such eagerness.

"Excuse me," Margaret muttered. "I must just deal with this."

Before she could storm over to the dance floor, Mr. Green was on his feet, shifting uneasily.

"You don't intend to intervene, do you, Miss Molyneaux? It would be rather shocking, you know. The dance will be over in a minute or two, anyway. Why not let it run its course?"

Margaret eyed the spinning couples with trepidation. She could see Marigold's golden head rotating in the middle of the crush, in the arms of a tall man with a face like an axe, leering down at her with nauseating intensity.

"No," she said decidedly. "I must do something."

She moved forward, or at least she would have, if a woman had not detached herself from the crowd and stepped in front of her, so abruptly that Margaret actually bumped into her.

Margaret's heart sank yet again. At this rate, she could expect her heart to do its beating from down in her boots.

"Lady Alice Bow," she stammered, backing away. "I did not see you there."

The woman in question shook out her skirts, straightened the heavy rope of pearls at her neck, and smiled at Margaret. It was not a pleasant smile.

"Heavens, Miss Molyneaux, how clumsy you are! I fear that you have stepped on the hem of my skirts. See, there is a tear."

Margaret who knew fine well that she had *not* stepped on the wretched woman's skirts, looked down anyway. Indeed, there was a small tear at the hem of the fine, emerald-green silk gown, about the length of a thumb.

"I fear I must ask you to pay for the cost of the gown," Lady Alice said, sighing in false regret. "Of course, I could just ask you to sew up the tear, but I think that would be rather humiliating, wouldn't it? I could *never* ask you to do such a thing."

Margaret allowed herself to imagine slapping Alice's perfectly proportioned face.

The fashion was for fair beauties at the moment, which meant that Alice's rich, flaxen curls and Marigold's golden hair were all the rage. Alice was tall, willowy, and pale, with pursed pink lips and large, fluttering blue eyes. She always knew what colours would suit her best, and her dresses were cut in the newest and most expensive styles, as colourful as possible.

Margaret was well aware that besides the likes of Lady Alice and her own younger sister, she resembled a modest sparrow next to a pair of flamboyant parrots. Margaret's hair was a light brown, thick and wavy but fairly ordinary, her eyes an unremarkable brown, her face even-featured but not brilliant, while her figure – well, there was no denying it. She was solidly built.

At least, that was what her mother had said, when the two girls were dressing for the party tonight.

"Try not to stand beside your sister too much, Margaret," she'd said, almost as an afterthought. "You'll look ugly if you do. What possessed you to choose that plum-coloured muslin? It quite drains you. Still, it's too late to change, and besides, everybody will be looking at Marigold anyway."

It was odd how words could burn into a person's brain and stay there, resurfacing at the worst moments. Such as now, for example.

"I haven't torn your gown, Lady Alice," Margaret said, lifting up her chin to look Lady Alice in the eye. "See how smooth the edges of the tear are, hardly frayed at all? It's been punctured by a heeled boot, I think. See, I am wearing dancing slippers. They are flat. The tear would be longer and ragged, if I had stepped on it."

Lady Alice's smirk dropped from her face. "Oh, of course, I should have known better than to argue with *you*, Miss Molyneaux. You're quite the scholar, if I remember rightly."

Mr. Green stepped forward, and Margaret immediately wished he had not.

"Oh, do you two ladies know each other?" he said, glancing nervously between them.

Alice hesitated, but only for a moment. Her eyes lit up, and a truly beautiful smile graced her face. She turned the full force of it on Mr. Green, who blinked and began to blush.

"We were at finishing school together, Mr. Green," she said, her voice light and melodious. That was the kind of skill the finishing school had taught – how to speak nicely. Margaret had never paid much attention.

Mr. Green was turning decidedly red. "Oh, how pleasant. You must be friends."

Friends? Margaret wanted to scream. *Why on earth do you think we should be friends? Haven't you been listening to any of this?*

"Indeed," Alice laughed, blinking slowly. She reached forward, laying a hand on his shoulder. "Now, I remember *you*, Arthur. Your father was a great friend of my father. I remember your older brothers chasing you around the attics when you were small, and locking you up in a trunk. Do you remember?"

"I do remember," Mr. Green said, laughing as if he hadn't just confided in Margaret how terrified he had always been of his older brothers. "Of course you were there – I'd quite forgotten. My older brother, Thomas, was quite in love with you. He used to tell anybody who would listen that he would marry you when he was older."

Alice threw her head back and laughed. It was a very ladylike laugh.

"Oh, how hilarious. Well, I only remember *you*, Mr. Green, presenting me with a little bouquet of daisies one day when I visited your family, when you were no older than eight or nine. Do you know, I think I still have them pressed in a book somewhere?"

Mr. Green's face lit up. "Truly? You kept them?"

Margaret turned away. It was painful to watch. She had seen Alice try this trick on a great many gentlemen. She knew how to be fascinating – another skill taught at their finishing school – and how to make a gentleman feel as though he were the most interesting creature alive. And while he believed that, well, they would do frankly anything for her.

On cue, the music stopped, and the dancers broke out in applause. There would be a moment's reprieve before the next melody commenced, and the flurry of parting with former partners to seek new ones would ensue.

"Oh, a new set is starting," Alice remarked, her tone calculatedly light. "I do so love to dance. Don't you, Mr. Green? Unfortunately, I have no partner."

This development was not a surprise to Margaret, but apparently it entirely bowled over Mr. Green. He hesitated, flushing red, clearly summoning up his courage.

"Would you care to dance, Lady Alice? I should hate for you not to be able to dance when you wished to do so."

Alice gave a pleased, surprised little exclamation, and threw a triumphant look over the man's shoulder at Margaret.

"Oh, Mr. Green, I should love to!"

He glanced apologetically at Margaret and handed over the half-finished lemonade.

"Do excuse me, Miss Molyneaux."

"Think nothing of it," she answered automatically, but the pair were already moving off towards the dance floor, arm in arm. Arthur shot one last glance at Margaret, and then the crowd swallowed him up.

Oh, well done, Alice, you have managed to get the last laugh once again, Margaret thought sourly, draining the lemonade. *But now you have to dance with him, don't you?*

She would tire of him soon enough, probably long before the dance ended. She would abandon him as soon as she could, secure in the knowledge that she could easily steal him away from Margaret, should the necessity arise. Mr. Green, shy again and feeling as though he had done something wrong, would make his way back to the seats, but Margaret would not be there when he arrived.

Margaret would have felt sorry for him, if all of her empathy wasn't being used up on herself. She had lost count of the times that Lady Alice had swooped in during a party and scooped some man away from Margaret.

A gentleman and a lady stepped out of the crowd, and Margaret shook herself out of her maudlin thoughts and hurried to meet them. The lady was trying to twist away, but the gentleman had her hand trapped in the crook of his arm.

"There you are, Marigold," Margaret said shortly, throwing a vague smile at the gentleman. "Here, I have some lemonade for you."

The man scowled at her. "Ah, you must be the sister. We haven't been introduced, so..."

"I am Miss Molyneaux," Margaret interrupted. "And I'm sure you needn't worry about us not being introduced, as I don't believe you were properly introduced to my sister either before you asked her to dance, Lord Tumnus."

He narrowed his eyes, and Marigold took the opportunity to whisk her hand out from his arm and came to stand beside her sister. She smiled gratefully up at her and drained the lemonade.

Marigold was already very much admired. She had had no proper coming-out party – they could not afford such a thing – but she was sweet, and beautiful, and formed like a perfect little doll, and apparently that was enough to put her on a level with all kinds of plainer heiresses.

Lord Tumnus sniffed, gaze raking Margaret up and down with visible disdain. "It's Margaret, is it not?"

Margaret kept a tight smile on her face. "It is Miss Molyneaux, actually."

"Goodness, your parents liked their *M* names, didn't they?"

"Very much so. We usually call my sister Goldie, though. If you'll excuse us…"

"Now, wait a moment. I'm going to fetch Miss Marigold here some refreshments, and we're going to sit and talk for a moment, aren't we?"

He smiled briefly down at Margaret, the smile never getting anywhere near his eyes.

She smiled too, equally insincere. "Oh, I think not, your lordship. I think Marigold wants to stay with me, don't you, dear?"

Marigold nodded earnestly.

"There you are, Lord Tumnus. Marigold needs to rest, and frankly I'm not sure that our mother would approve of…"

"Actually," he interrupted – quite a rude thing to do, interrupting a lady, although Margaret was used to small slights like that by now – "It was your mother, Lady Keswick, who introduced us to start with."

A cold sensation crept down Margaret's spine, and she glanced down at her sister, eyebrows raised questioningly. Marigold gave the tiniest nod.

"I see," Margaret managed, voice tight. "Well, thank you for taking care of Marigold for a while, Lord Tumnus. We shan't keep you any longer."

She didn't wait for him to argue or to insist. Instead, Margaret simply tightened her arm through Marigold's and towed her sister off into the crowd. Her heart pounded for a moment or two, until she assured herself that they were not being followed and allowed herself a breath of relief.

"Thank you, Maggie," Marigold whispered, voice tight. "I don't like him. He makes me feel… he scares me, Margaret. I didn't like how he looked at me. It was like he was hungry."

Margaret shivered. "Well, you're safe with me, you know that. But what was Mama thinking of when she decided to introduce you to him?"

"I don't know, but I want to go home. Will you ask Mama if we can go home, Maggie?"

"I shall *tell* Mama that we are going home," Margaret corrected firmly. "Just stay with me, and we'll find her."

"Thank you, Maggie. What happened to Mr. Green, by the way? He seemed very nice. I thought he liked you."

"So did I, until Lady Alice Bow appeared and charmed him away."

Marigold pulled a face. "I *hate* that woman."

"You, my dear, are too sweet to hate anyone. Lady Alice has a grudge against me, that's for sure."

Marigold frowned. "But what did you do to make her so angry at you?"

Margaret shook her head, sighing. "I haven't the slightest idea, Goldie, not the slightest idea."

Chapter Two

The carriage ride home was cold, in more ways than one.

Goldie, wrapped in rugs and exhausted from dancing all night, fell asleep quickly, her head resting against Margaret's shoulder.

"We should have stayed longer," Lady Keswick said, voice flat and emotionless.

Margaret glanced over at her mother. "Goldie's tired. It was the right time to leave."

"If you say so."

Lady Keswick was a remarkably good-looking woman for her age, and the rich black velvet of her mourning clothes only seemed to improve her figure and face. She was tall and graceful, with none of the stockiness that afflicted her oldest daughter. She had sharp, beautiful features, and an air of authority that seemed to make crowds part for her.

Or at least, it *had* done, before her husband died of a sudden apoplexy and left the Molyneaux house notably low on its finances. Lady Keswick had not seen fit to burden her daughters with the details, but Margaret was not a fool.

"You ought not to call her *Goldie* in public, you know," Lady Keswick suddenly said. "It's a rather childish nickname."

Margaret bristled. "Mama, she *is* a child."

"Nonsense. Marigold might be married by the end of the year, a woman grown."

"She doesn't wish to marry yet."

Lady Keswick turned to look out of the window, although it was dark outside and surely all she could see would be her reflection, pale and hazy and staring back.

"I have been meaning to speak to you about something rather serious, Margaret, and I suppose that now is the best time."

This was not a good sign. Drawing in a deep breath, Margaret steeled herself. At least Goldie was asleep and would not have to overhear anything troublesome. Margaret knew that her younger sister was fragile and tended towards anxiety. She was kind and wanted to alleviate everybody's suffering all of the time.

Regrettably, the world was not fashioned in such a manner. Gentle and amiable young ladies like Goldie were often devoured and discarded, or at the very least, subjected to the advances of gentlemen like Lord Tumnus.

Who, apparently, had been introduced by Lady Keswick herself.

No, this "conversation" would be nothing good, Margaret was sure about that.

Lady Keswick took her time, fidgeting with her gloves and cuffs. For a moment, Margaret wondered whether her mother was actually *nervous*.

"It's no secret that your father left us in a dire predicament," she blurted out, quite suddenly. "The money is all but gone, and that's before we take into account the debts he racked up. Your father was not a bad man, or a cruel one, but he was certainly foolish. There's no dowry for you girls, not a penny. There is some money set aside for me, as a widow, but not much. Not enough to save us."

Margaret swallowed. "I had guessed as much."

Lady Keswick passed a hand over her face, and Margaret realised with a jolt that her mother's hand was shaking.

"You are very clever, aren't you, Margaret?"

She flinched. It didn't sound like a compliment.

"Always *guessing*, always figuring things out," Lady Keswick continued, a definite hint of bitterness creeping into her voice. "Well, let me tell you this. If you were pretty rather than clever, then perhaps you might have made a great match and saved us all. As it is, you can barely hold on to Arthur Green, the most unimportant son of a mediocre house. An offer from him..."

"...is not likely," Margaret interrupted. She wasn't entirely sure what drove her to say as much, only that her mother was likely to find out sooner or later, and it was probably best to just get it over with. "Lady Alice Bow took him away, and I fancy he'll be dreaming of her for a while now."

Not that Alice would think twice about a man like Arthur Green, even if he was too foolish to see it. Margaret felt sorry for him, even though she should probably keep her pity for herself.

"Wonderful," Lady Keswick said, voice heavy and tired. "Well, Margaret, you are nearly three-and-twenty and have never been beautiful. You are clever, although that does not particularly work in your favour. You have never applied yourself to catching a man's attention, and it's too late to try now. I think it's fair to assume that you are destined for spinsterhood."

Margaret avoided her mother's eye and picked at her skirts. It was last year's dress, the plum-coloured muslin, and seemed to suit her worse than it had then. There were a few discreet darns on the hem, but they could not afford to replace the gown. New gowns for Margaret were a waste, anyway. As Lady Keswick had reminded her frequently, nobody would look at her.

"I think so, too," she said at last, when it was clear that some response was expected. "And we have years before Goldie can be expected to make a decent match. If we can just..."

"Not necessarily," Lady Keswick interrupted. "There is a gentleman very interested in Marigold at the moment. She can marry at once, you know. Seventeen is not so very young."

There was a moment of silence between them.

"I hope you do not mean Lord Tumnus," Margaret said at last, voice strained.

Lady Keswick had the grace to look embarrassed. "He's a rich man, Margaret. He doesn't care that Marigold has no dowry. He might seriously consider marriage with her."

A wave of nausea rushed over her, making Margaret genuinely afraid that she might vomit up the mixture of champagne, lemonade, and biscuits that were all she'd eaten in the past few hours.

"You cannot let Goldie marry that man," she managed at last. "You can't. He's... he's awful. Didn't you hear that rumour about him and some poor, friendless girl out in the country? He's a monster!"

Lady Keswick sighed. "Men are just like that, Margaret."

"She was fifteen!"

"Girls mature faster, my dear, you know that."

"Nonsense. Nonsense!"

"Keep your voice down," Lady Keswick hissed, nodding at Goldie. "Unless you want to wake up your sister and discuss it with her. She is not of age, and I am her mother, and that means I shall decide what is best for her. I have a legal and a moral right to do so."

"You cannot believe that Lord Tumnus is going to be *the best* for her," Margaret hissed. "Even you could not believe that. Goldie is terrified of him, don't you see?"

"And what would you have me do, Margaret? It's not as if you are going to save us all. I don't think you understand just how close we are to disaster. It's not simply a case of having no money anymore. We are *destitute*. Despite having let go most of the servants and selling off all the land we can, while we can, we are going to lose the house. Your father's creditors are drawing near, much like hawks surveying their territory, and it won't be long before one of them takes decisive action. Once they sense an opportunity, the situation could deteriorate rapidly. And then, Marigold will be vulnerable, and prey to far worse men than Lord Tumnus. I can assure you that there *are* worse men than him, and you will have no way of defending her from them."

Lady Keswick fell silent after this impassioned speech, spots of colour burning in her usually white cheeks. She sat back against the carriage seats, staring blankly out of the window.

Margaret found that she was holding her breath, and a pain was spreading across her chest. A headache throbbed between her temples, and she felt sicker than ever. It could be a combination of the sickly lemonade and her own tension, or it could have been the jerking and rattling of the carriage. The coach was in dire need of re-springing, as well as reupholstering, a thorough scrubbing, and a proper re-lacquering. Alas, they found themselves lacking the funds to undertake even a fraction of these necessary repairs.

"I see," Margaret said at last. "It doesn't seem fair that we're left to deal with Papa's debts."

Lady Keswick shrugged. "It isn't fair, but the money and land were all his. Now that he's dead, his creditors have the right to take a piece of the estate before it passes to us. We're women, my dear. We don't really own anything, not even ourselves."

Goldie shifted against Margaret's shoulder, sighing in her sleep. Margaret's heart clenched.

Not my sister, she thought, feeling ill. *I can't let this happen to her. I have to save her. I must save her. Nobody else will.*

I can't save her.

"So what do you propose?" Margaret said at last. "We push Goldie at Lord Tumnus, who may or may not deign to marry her?"

Lady Keswick was quiet for a long moment after that.

"Not exactly," she said at last. "Not yet. Only a few hours before we left, I received *this*," she withdrew a letter from her reticule, holding it up in something like triumph.

"And what does it say?" Margaret asked tiredly. She was thoroughly sick of her mother's sense of drama.

"Let me give you a little context. One of your father's creditors has written to me about the debt, seeking repayment. As he is – apparently – a gentleman, I thought I might try and throw myself on his mercy. I explained the situation, and waited to see what would happen."

"A true gentleman wouldn't chase a man's widow and daughters to reclaim a debt," Margaret snapped.

Her mother continued as if she had not spoken. "Imagine my surprise and curiosity when the gentleman wrote back, requesting to meet with me

– and both of you – to discuss the matter further. He says – and I quote – that a *mutually beneficial arrangement* might be met."

Lady Keswick sat back, smiling triumphantly. A sense of unease prickled in Margaret's gut.

"That could mean anything. It could mean that he thinks we have valuable things in our home, or that he is our only creditor. He might be less of a gentleman than you think and have some nefarious scheme in mind."

"*Nefarious scheme*? Goodness, Margaret, you read entirely too many novels. Still, I happen to know that this gentleman is single, and a *duke*. Imagine if he were to fall in love with Marigold?"

Margaret sighed. "Well, *that* isn't likely to happen, is it?"

Her mother sniffed. "Stranger things have happened. Men of his calibre, my dear, do not need to marry rich women. Why should he not marry the pretty, young little thing?"

"Because Goldie is a child, Mama."

Lady Keswick shook her head. "Not in the eyes of many men, my dear."

That was an unsettling thought, and Margaret stayed quiet for a while after that. Only ten minutes later, they reached home.

***

Molyneaux Manor had once been a very fine place, the pinnacle of fashion and good taste. Of course, that was back when Margaret assumed that everything in her home was properly paid for, properly *owned* by them.

She was wrong about that. Only days after the funeral, the house had been stripped of its valuable things, which it turned out they had never properly owned at all. Lady Keswick had rushed around the house in a mad dash, trying to collect the things she wished to save before they could be taken by blank-faced men with notebooks. They marked off everything they took, noting its value beside.

Now, the place was emptier than before, dustier than before, and noticeably quieter. They hadn't entertained since before Lord Molyneaux died.

Margaret was vaguely aware that she ought to miss her father, but then again, it wasn't as if she'd seen very much of him before he died, except at the occasional suppertime. At times, it felt as though he'd never been there at all.

Goldie was put to bed almost immediately, yawning and stretching and entirely unaware of the conversation which had gone on over her head, about her future and theirs.

Upstairs, Margaret retreated to her own bedchamber. She had no lady's maid, of course. The head housemaid used to do her hair and Goldie's, and take care of their clothes, but the woman had put in her notice months ago, citing unpaid wages. Margaret felt guilty over that. She had gone to her jewellery box, intending to take something to sell to pay Lucy's owed wages, only to find that the box was empty.

Her mother had taken it all, half a year ago, and admitted to it freely. They had had a shouting match over that.

She undressed quickly, shivering in her night things in front of the empty grate. Firewood, of course, was expensive, and not to be wasted on bedroom warmth. She would warm up quickly enough once she was in bed.

Margaret did not, however, get into bed right away. After a moment's thought, she seized her candle and ventured out into the dark hallway. Almost all of the lights were off, except for her mother's room at the end of the corridor, a beam of light making its way out into the hall.

Lady Keswick sat at her dressing table, applying a cold cream to her cheeks. She glanced briefly at Margaret in the mirror.

"Not asleep yet? I thought you were exhausted; you were so keen to come home. Did you want to borrow some of my cream? It's very good for the skin. Very smoothing, very whitening," she paused, glancing over at Margaret again. "You could certainly benefit from a night-time cream, I think. Some cream, or perhaps a powder..."

"I'm here to talk about that creditor," Margaret interrupted. "I assume you've already told him to meet us."

"You are right. He is coming tomorrow, so I expect Marigold and you to wear your nicest gowns and to be on your best behaviour."

"You truly think he'll agree to a deal? Even if he does, we'll still have other creditors to worry about."

Lady Keswick shrugged. "It's an opportunity, is it not? I think he may be willing to help us because... well, because he's a rather odd man. I don't believe he's been in Society these last few years, and he had a reputation as being somewhat harsh."

"Then how do you know he won't demand his money at once and throw us out?"

Lady Keswick screwed the cap back onto her little pot of cream, turning her face this way and that to admire her skin. She gave a small pout into the mirror, and Margaret was reminded for the thousandth time that her mother had been described as a Great Beauty when she was young.

"He is unpredictable, from what I have heard," she continued, thoughtfully. "I think that if he was simply going to demand his money back from us, he would have sent bailiffs and collectors to do so. I believe he's done so in the past. This meeting *means* something, Margaret. It isn't a formality, or a courtesy. He's not a man given to either. He wants something from us, and it's not the money we owe him. I, for one, want to find out what it is."

Margaret swallowed hard. Suddenly, it seemed colder than before, her nightdress even thinner and more flimsy than when she'd left the bedroom. The wooden floor was ice cold under her bare feet.

"Who is he, then, Mama? What's his name?"

Lady Keswick sighed. "I imagine you've heard of him. It's the Duke of Stonehaven."

Chapter Three

The closer they got to Molyneaux Manor, the more potholed the road seemed to become. The grass verges were overgrown, waist-high with weeds, and if there had ever been any gravel on the ground, he would wager it hadn't been raked in *years*.

Sighing, Jasper leaned back against the carriage seat.

This is a mistake.

The thought had occurred, quite often, over the journey here. He suspected if the meeting had been scheduled for tomorrow instead of today, he might have cancelled it altogether.

That, no doubt, was probably why Lady Keswick had suggested they meet so soon.

He couldn't remember the woman in question, although apparently their paths had crossed in Society before. He had, of course, heard of the Molyneaux family, and their recent financial troubles. He remembered the debt, but it had not seemed important to claim it back right away. It wasn't as if he needed the money.

As far as he could recall, Lady Keswick had not been a friend of his mother's, and her husband had not been liked or respected by his father, so they had never really shared the same circles.

Perhaps that was for the best.

The old Duke of Stonehaven had been dead for seven years, and the Duchess dead for five. Being an orphan suited Jasper – he was not sure he had ever really been anything else. He wished, not for the first time, that he had brought John.

His steward was the one who had brought Lady Keswick's pleading letter to his attention, reading it out carefully. He suspected that John had some chivalrous ideas of Jasper forgiving the debt altogether, to the gratitude of a widow and her fatherless daughters.

He ought to have known better, Jasper thought grimly. *Father always told me never do anything for nothing, and it's a good piece of advice.*

Still, it would have been good to have John here, with his easy manners and quick wit. There might be things to read, too.

Jasper's heart sank at that, but he did not allow himself to dwell on the subject.

The house in question appeared in the distance, and he pulled back the curtain of the carriage window to peer out.

Ramshackle, dilapidated, ugly, old-fashioned, he thought, with resignation. *It's barely worth enough to cover their debts, I'd warrant. Once everything is paid off, they'll have pennies to their names.*

Perhaps he ought to have felt pity, but as Jasper well knew, pity was a finite thing, and it was always best to keep it all for oneself.

As he was considering this, a movement inside the carriage caught his eye.

It was a moth, a delicate, grey-winged thing, fluttering around in a panic. It headed for the window, butting its minute head against the glass again and again, leaving almost imperceptible sprays of dust.

Sighing, Jasper captured the thing in his two hands, carefully not to crush it, or touch the delicate wings. With impeccable timing, the carriage rolled to a halt. He waited for a minute, until the footman on the back of the carriage hurried to open the door, and then he could release the moth into the fresh morning air.

"Molyneaux Manor, Your Grace," the footman said, never batting an eyelid at the newly freed insect.

Jasper climbed out of the carriage, straightening cramped limbs, and took a look around.

He could see curtains twitching behind the great front windows of the house, and there was no doubt that he was being watched.

Still, he took his time, stretching and looking around.

Carriage journeys were never pleasant, especially not for a man of his size. Jasper had been small and slight at age twelve, but only three or four years later a growth spurt shot him up to beyond six feet, easily six and a half, with broad shoulders and a powerful chest, the sort of chest that all men wanted to achieve. He never gave much consideration to his clothes, but today he had allowed John to choose a suitable outfit, with a silk waistcoat and a nicely tied cravat.

Aside from that, he had not bothered with pomade or anything to style his black hair, and even though he had shaved that morning, it was likely there was a blue-black tinge to his jaw already. Often, he thought about just giving up altogether, and growing a beard instead of shaving twice a day.

And then he decided that he had done enough and turned towards the large front door of the house. A wide-eyed butler showed him through narrow halls, and he was ushered into a large, comfortable parlour.

It wasn't much like the Blue Parlour, and that was a relief.

Three women waited for him there, rising to their feet when he entered.

No, two women and a girl. Lady Keswick came forward to greet him, of course, but Jasper's gaze slipped straight past her to look at the daughters. He hadn't had much information about them, except that one was older and one was younger, and the youngest one was clearly still a child, which was disappointing.

"Your Grace," Lady Keswick said, sinking into a graceful curtsey which her daughters mirrored. "I have already rung for tea. Pray, be seated."

She gestured to a wide armchair behind him, and he sat, slowly and carefully.

The three females sat in unison, all three looking at him.

Lady Keswick cleared her throat. "Your Grace, I don't believe you've met my daughter, Miss Marigold?"

Jasper had expected to be introduced to the older daughter, but to his surprise, it was the younger one that stepped forward. He bounced to his feet, taking her tiny hand in his. She was clearly terrified, staring up at him as if he were going to harm her. He opened his mouth to say something polite and reassuring. Unfortunately, what came out was somewhat otherwise.

"Shouldn't she be in the schoolroom?"

The girl Miss Marigold cringed. "No, Your Grace," she whispered, eyes nearly popping out of her head. "I'm quite grown."

He stared down at her, noting that her head did not even come to the middle of his chest.

"Grown? I think not. Lady Keswick, perhaps we should let your youngest girl go about her business and let us three adults talk instead."

Lady Keswick pressed her lips together. "Your Grace, I really..."

"An excellent idea, Mama. His Grace is right. Go on, Goldie, go read your book. It's quite alright."

It was the other daughter that answered, rising briskly to her feet and shooing her sister away as if she feared for her life. He stood, shifting uncomfortably from foot to foot, and eyed the woman who had spoken.

He guessed that she was about three-and-twenty, built like a grown woman instead of those willowy beauties that seemed to be wafting around these days, with a straight spine and a firm, unblinking gaze. She was pretty, he thought, in a brisk, no-nonsense sort of way.

The door closed behind poor Miss Marigold, and the older daughter took matters into her own hands.

"I am Miss Molyneaux," she said brusquely, dropping a brief curtsey. "Your Grace, permit me to be direct."

"Margaret!" her mother exclaimed, vaguely horrified, but the girl ploughed on regardless.

"Our father died owing you a significant amount of money, correct? In your letter, you implied to my mother that we might come to some arrangement."

Jasper bit the inside of his cheek. He had not, of course, seen the letter. John had read it out to him once the dictation and writing was finished, and he had signed the bottom, but that was all. He knew that John wouldn't add or take away anything he should not, but the fear was sometimes still there.

"That is correct, yes," he said aloud, instead of voicing these concerns. Miss Molyneaux let out a long, slow breath, and glanced at her mother.

Lady Keswick glanced at him, eyebrows raised, and it occurred to Jasper that the time had come to make his suggestion.

The idea had come to him rather suddenly, and he had dismissed it at once. But it returned, again and again, in that unkillable way that ideas often had, until it made absolute, perfect sense.

And yet, now that he was here and ready to actually say it aloud, he felt uncharacteristically afraid.

Come on, Jasper. Nobody will do a thing for you in this life, you know that.

"I believe that my reputation may have preceded me, ladies," he said at last.

Lady Keswick gave a nervous chuckle. "Why, no, Your Grace, we…"

"Yes," Miss Molyneaux interrupted, ignoring the furious look her mother shot her way. "Indeed, we have heard of you, Your Grace. People speak of you."

He leaned back in his chair. "And what do they say?"

To her credit, she did not flinch.

"You are not a sociable man. You don't enjoy Society, and never join the Season. You're said to be harsh, unpleasant, and bad-tempered. I hope this does not offend you, Your Grace."

He shrugged. "It is foolish to be offended at the truth, don't you think?"

She said nothing, only waited for him to continue. He cleared his throat and pressed on.

"Well, as I said, my reputation has preceded me, so I imagine it will be of no surprise to you to know that I am not a well-liked man. I have few friends, have never pursued an engagement, and yet I have a dukedom to manage and a vast estate to run. The matter of your debt to me – or, should I say, the late Lord Keswick's debt – reminded me of something important

– that is, that the mess we leave of our lives can pass on to those who come after us."

It was a rather good speech, he thought, but Miss Molyneaux only stared flatly at him.

"What are you trying to say, Your Grace?" she said at last. This time, her mother didn't even bother glare at her. She just sat there, looking mortified.

Frankly, Jasper preferred her bluntness. It was easier to just *say* things, to get them out of the way without all of the nonsense and folly that people seemed to think was necessary beforehand. Miss Molyneaux seemed like a good, sensible sort of woman. She was also very pretty, or at least, he thought so. Prettiness was neither here nor there, of course, but he did find that his gaze was drawn back to her more often than he would like.

"I need a wife, Miss Molyneaux," he said, without further ado. "Most high Society ladies would not look at me twice, and I have no taste for courtship in any case. So, I thought I might look for a more... practical arrangement."

There. He had said it.

A silence washed over the room. Lady Keswick looked as though she could not decide whether to be delighted or horrified. Miss Molyneaux's face was carefully impassive.

"And if we do not agree to your suggestion, you'll call in our debt?" Miss Molyneaux said, barely concealed anger simmering beneath her words.

He snorted. "Hardly. I'm not a monster. I intend to write off your debt, as a sort of goodwill gesture. I don't need the money, and you have creditors enough to ruin you without me. But should we reach an arrangement, it would of course be my responsibility to buy up this estate and its debts, which would keep you all safe from financial disgrace and provide a comfortable life."

Miss Molyneaux opened her mouth to speak, but her mother hastily interrupted.

"Just a moment. I shall summon Miss Marigold at once. She..."

He held up a hand for silence, and she trailed off.

"I do not intend to marry a child, Lady Keswick."

She flushed red. "Marigold is seventeen."

"Like I said," he answered shortly. "A child. I need a duchess for a number of reasons, not least of all managing my house and ultimately helping me raise at least one heir. For that, I need a grown woman. Miss Marigold seems pleasant enough, but she is not what I am looking for."

29

There was a heavy pause in the room, during which both Lady Keswick's gaze and Jasper's turned to Miss Molyneaux.

She was sitting very stiffly in her seat, a frown between her brows.

"Am I to understand," she said carefully, "that you are proposing *marriage* to *me*?"

Why did that seem to be such a ludicrous idea to her? No doubt she had plenty of suitors in Society – she was pretty and seemed clever and interesting – but he doubted that any of them were *dukes*.

"Exactly," he answered shortly. "A marriage of convenience."

She gave a wry little smile. "Indeed, you made that clear. And were there no other options for you, Your Grace?"

He paused, considering. John had presented several suitable ladies for him, once he explained that he wanted a *practical* marriage, but Jasper had not got as far as contacting any of them. And then Lady Keswick's letter had arrived, and it had really seemed like fate.

"Of course," he answered, a trifle defensively. "But a lot of ladies tend to want at least the semblance of courtship. Some families would be rather offended if I were to propose such a thing. I had thought, that if you were offended, my writing off the debt would convince you not to talk too much about the matter."

There. Honesty. People liked honesty, didn't they?

Apparently not. Lady Keswick baulked, visibly offended.

"Your Grace, I must protest. To imagine that I and my daughters are common gossips, who would bandy your good name around London..." she trailed off, giving a gesture that seemed to indicate that she simply was overwhelmed.

He blinked, wondering if he was meant to say anything else. An apology, perhaps? But then, he had not really done anything wrong.

Before Lady Keswick could say something further, or perhaps faint – she was looking very pale – Miss Molyneaux spoke again.

"If I were to accept your offer," she said, musingly, "I would be your wife. I would run your house, support you in Society..."

"You may have to introduce me to Society. Not that I intend to go in it much, but my business matters are increasingly forcing me into Society again. My estate must not be allowed to suffer."

She cleared her throat. "I'm sure I can do that. I can make a financial plan comply, I can..."

"You won't need to do that. I have plenty of money."

She shot him an annoyed glance, and it occurred to Jasper just a moment too late that gentlemen were not supposed to interrupt ladies.

"And what do you offer, Your Grace?" she said at last. "You'll forgive our debt, and buy up the estate, so you can be considered to have bought me, body and soul."

He did not like that idea and hoped that his face showed it.

"You don't need to lay it all out like that," he snapped. "Marriage is transactional by nature, is it not?"

"Certainly, it is. Not quite so bluntly as this, though."

He'd had enough. Jasper got to his feet, just as the door was pushed open and a pale-faced maid appeared with a tea tray.

"It's clear that you are offended," he said shortly. "I should not have said any of this. I beg your forgiveness, and I will leave immediately."

He turned to go, but stopped dead at the sound of Miss Molyneaux's voice.

"Wait."

He paused, glancing over his shoulder. She was on her feet, face pale, spots of colour burning in the middle of her cheeks. He lifted his eyebrows.

She drew in a breath. "As well as paying off our debts, I want a dowry for my sister. I want to be able to take care of her."

"Margaret!" Lady Keswick hissed.

Jasper did not blink. "Done." he said shortly.

She swallowed hard. "Then I agree. I shall marry you."

Chapter Four

Polite Society and the readers of this journal, the Gazelle, *have been shocked by the sudden, unheralded engagement of the famously reclusive Duke of Stonehaven. His bride is none other than Miss Margaret Molyneaux, a young woman unremarkable in Society and not regarded a beauty. The Molyneaux fortunes are, as have been reported upon by this author in this journal, not doing well.*

Which, we know well, is the polite term of saying that the Molyneaux family is on Destitution's Doorstep. This marriage to the Duke will certainly be a good thing for Miss Molyneaux, and for her family, which includes a younger sister of great beauty and, it is said, great sweetness. If she were to add a respectable dowry to her charms, this author thinks that Miss Marigold Molyneaux may well take Society by storm in another year or two.

So, can our dear readers expect a detailed description of this notorious marriage?

This author cannot say, as the wedding is meanly small, with few invited persons. Shall this author be in the fleet? Perhaps, perhaps not.

Either way, we shall look with great interest on the progress of Miss Molyneaux – soon to be the Duchess of Stonehaven – as she progresses through Society. The Duke, as mentioned before, is famously reclusive, known for his brusque manners, bad temper, and general ungentlemanly behaviour. Can this sudden marriage mean that the beastly Duke intends to return to Society? Who only knows? Only time shall tell whether Miss Molyneaux can tame this beast, or whether she will become yet another tale of unfulfilled dreams, as so many have done before her.

Either way, what excitement! What gossip! What <u>news</u>! We in Society are voraciously hungry for excitement, and by Heaven, do we find it. Today, all eyes are on Miss Molyneaux, and her mysterious, beastly husband.

Good luck, Miss Margaret Molyneaux. You shall need it.

There were countless scandal sheets roaming around London, in varying levels of popularity. Some – like the *Gazelle*, a parody journal of the *Gazette* and full of well-written, tongue-in-cheek gossip – were read by just about everybody, staples on every coffee-table and breakfast table. Others were a little more obscure, their information vaguer and slacker on details and evidence.

Almost all of them, however, had mentioned the Duke of Stonehaven and his mysterious bride.

Only, Margaret was not mysterious, was she? She had never hidden the fact of their engagement. Many journals had immediately pointed out that the two had never come face to face in a social setting, so how could their courtship had been carried out?

This was true, but Margaret itched to point out that *nobody* had come face to face with the duke in a good long while, due to him living practically as a hermit in his fine, distant estate.

Marriages of convenience were, mostly, the norm, no matter what the novels and scandal sheets liked to claim. How often had a couple coldly courted each other for a month or two, rigidly counting out the days before an engagement could be announced? An engagement which, everybody knew, had been decided upon almost before the couple met for the first time.

No, the only difference was that Margaret's marriage was so *clearly* arranged.

Perhaps that's why they don't like it, she thought, inspecting her face in the mirror. *I've stripped away the lies and nonsense that others consider necessary, and they won't forgive me for it.*

It hardly mattered. Today was the day. Her *wedding* day.

Margaret stared at her own face again, until her features blurred.

Lady Keswick was off somewhere, shouting at servants and bothering about details that were not worth bothering about.

The wedding was, of course, to be held at Stonehaven Manor. The duke had expressed a wish to have the ceremony on his own property, and their house was too embarrassing to invite guests.

Goldie wrapped her arms around Margaret's shoulders from behind, pressing a kiss to her sister's temple.

"You look beautiful, Margaret."

Margaret smiled weakly. "It hardly matters, does it? I am not here to be beautiful. I am here to get married and fulfil a contractual obligation. It's the ideas of romance novels, is it not?", she added ironically.

Goldie sighed. "At least *try* to enjoy your day. Look, I have a present for you."

Margaret scowled. "I hope you haven't spent your precious little money on gifts for me. I am going to be a duchess soon enough."

"I did not buy it, I borrowed it," Goldie responded. She didn't offer any more details, and Margaret wasn't sure she wanted to ask.

Her sister withdrew a delicate brooch, shaped like a kingfisher, its shimmering blue stones reminiscent of sapphires and set against a ring of polished silver. It was undoubtedly beautiful, far finer than any adornment Margaret had owned in quite some time.

She smiled, swallowing back a lump in her throat. "Oh, it's lovely, Goldie. Why don't you keep it for yourself?"

"No, it must reflect Your Grace, your charm, and your spirit all at once," Goldie responded firmly, pinning the brooch to Margaret's bodice.

The dress had been bought with some money the duke had carelessly given to Lady Keswick, almost as an afterthought. The dress was a very pale blue, shot through with silver, with pearls and sequins glittering on a too-tight bodice that was all the rage at the moment. The neckline was square, and Margaret's hair had been elaborately curled and piled onto the top of her head, a few ringlets allowed to fall artfully down onto her neck.

In short, Margaret did not feel like herself at all. She *did* look beautiful, though.

Well, perhaps *pretty*. One couldn't have everything, after all.

She stared at herself in the mirror again, lifting a hand to trace the outline of the kingfisher brooch.

"Do you like it?" Goldie asked, a tremble of anxiety in her voice.

Margaret turned, wrapping her arms around her sister.

"Of course, I like it. Of *course*, I like it. In fact, I love it."

"I'm glad. And I'm glad that I'm staying with you after the wedding, Margaret. I know your honeymoon is only two weeks long, but I shall miss you so, so dreadfully."

Margaret tightened her grip. "It's only two weeks. Only fourteen days, think of it like that. And then you shall move into lovely chambers here at the Manor, and men like Lord Tumnus will never bother you again. I shall be a duchess, and they will *have* to defer to me."

Goldie's expression brightened. "You are the best sister in the world. And the duke had better treat you nicely, or else I shall put poison in his wine."

"Oh, hush, you wretched girl! Poison, indeed! Your education will be the death of me."

"It's quite all right, sister. I was jesting.

Margaret decided not to ask any further questions about her sister's murderous future plans. It was to be hoped that the poor duke wouldn't give any reasons to unleash Goldie's newfound bloodlust.

"By the way, I've sent some of his Grace's servants to collect your things from home," Margaret said. "So that you when you come here after the honeymoon, everything will be ready for you to settle in."

Their conversation was interrupted by the door banging open. Lady Keswick stamped in, looking bad-tempered.

"Barely fifty guests," she muttered sourly. "I am mortified. Margaret, are you ready? You are getting married in half an hour. We should go."

Panic rippled down Margaret's spine. She turned to look one more time at the unfamiliar face greeting her in the mirror and swallowed deeply.

This is it. I'm getting married. I'm getting married to a man I have met exactly once, and exchanged a handful of letters with.

I must be mad.

"I'm ready," she heard herself say, voice surprisingly cool and collected. She rose to her feet, pausing only to adjust the kingfisher brooch on her bodice.

***

The wedding, as the scandal sheets would later report, was nothing very interesting. There were no shocking statements given aloud at the ceremony, nobody tried to stop the wedding, nobody tried to run. Margaret did not faint, or cry, or claim to have been forced into the marriage. She just stood quietly by the altar, beside her hulking husband-to-be, and responded properly to the vicar's prompts.

At the end, the vicar did indeed request the bride and groom to kiss. Margaret barely had time to panic before her brand-new husband huffed in annoyance, then bent down and hastily pressed a quick, stubbly kiss to her cheek, so quickly she thought she might have imagined it.

Then it was over, they were married, and Margaret was reeling. She held the duke's hand carefully, only her extreme fingertips resting on the back of his knuckles, and they led the guests from the chapel into the expanse of the main house, where the table was set for the wedding breakfast.

And then, without so much as a word or a glance in her direction, her brand-new husband disappeared.

I'm a married woman. I am a married woman. I am a duchess, Margaret thought, over and over again, mechanically smiling and receiving congratulations, circling the busy dining room and wondering what on earth she was meant to do next.

The table was set, the guests were engaged in bright conversation, and the presence of good wine, excellent food, and expensive champagne had gone a long way to soothing the guests' offence at the groom's disappearance.

"Miss Moly... uh, I suppose it is *Your Grace* now, forgive me," came an unfamiliar, Irish-tinged voice. She turned to see a round-faced, smiling man of middling height, possibly just short of thirty years old. He bowed, and she made a curtsey before she could stop herself.

"You cannot curtsey to me, Your Grace," the man said, laughing. "You are now the Duchess of Stonehaven. There are not many people you curtsey too."

"It will take some getting used to," Margaret admitted, smiling despite herself. The man had warm, kindly air about him, and she began to feel relaxed.

"My name is John Locke, am I his Grace's steward. I came to make his apologies, actually. He's gone to see about some business on his estates."

Margaret frowned. "On his wedding day? It's our wedding breakfast."

Did John know about the circumstances of their marriage? She was willing to bet he did.

John winced, avoiding her eye. "I know, Your Grace. I am sorry."

Margaret nodded, clearing her throat, and half-turned away. "Well, I am glad you told me. If you'll excuse..."

"He's a good man," John said suddenly, then flushed at his own daring. She glanced back at him, and he reluctantly met her gaze.

"He is a good man, the duke," John said at last. "I've known him for years. It's not for me to say, of course, but you've chosen a good husband, Your Grace."

Margaret blinked, not entirely sure what to say in response to that.

"It wasn't exactly my choice," she said at last.

John bit his lip. "I know, Your Grace. I know."

There seemed to be nothing to say after that, and the two of them parted ways.

Margaret wandered through the rooms, wishing she had more of an appetite, forcing smiles at passing guests. There was still no sign of her husband, and she was beginning to realize that he had made his escape from the wedding breakfast on purpose.

Why? Why does he avoid Society? Why is he so sharp and strange? He's not mad, is he? The journals called him a beast. Is there some hideous secret about him I don't know?

Margaret shivered. No answers were forthcoming, and she certainly wasn't going to tramp around the house and estate trying to find them. Not today, at least. With a little effort, she recalled her husband's first name. She couldn't possibly go through their marriage calling him *Your Grace* or referring to him as *the Duke*.

"Jasper," she murmured. "His name is Jasper."

She was in the middle of her reflections when her mother came barrelling out of the crowd, red-faced, and stormed over to her.

"Some of that man's servants have been in our house, taking my things!" Lady Keswick hissed, outraged.

I am too tired for this.

"Do you perhaps mean that they took Goldie's things?"

Lady Keswick faltered. "Well, I mean, they did take things that only Goldie uses, but since she is a child and I am her mother, then really…"

"I sent them, Mama. I wanted Goldie's things here and ready for when she moves in after the honeymoon. If there is anything you need in the meantime, simply let me know and I'll have it returned at once."

Lady Keswick blinked at that, pressing her lips together. There was a taut silence, and Margaret knew before the silence was broken that the conversation was not going to go well.

"About this business of Marigold living with you," Lady Keswick said carefully, "I am not sure it's in her best interests."

Margaret stiffened. "We agreed on it, Mama. You said she could live with me. I invited *you* to live with us, if you recall, and you said no."

Lady Keswick waved a hand dismissively. "I am Goldie's mother, so I think she had better stay with me, after all."

"She wants to come with me," Margaret insisted, heart starting to pound.

I might have known that she wouldn't let Goldie go so easily.

"Why don't we talk about it after the honeymoon?" Lady Keswick said, smiling tightly. "I would have stopped the servants from taking Goldie's things, only that wretched housekeeper of the duke's got in the way. She is a most impertinent, frosty sort of woman."

"I haven't met his housekeeper yet."

My housekeeper, Margaret corrected herself.

Lady Keswick sniffed. "Mrs. Nettle, that's her name. What a silly name. Anyway, I shall let you enjoy your wedding party, dear. Where is your husband, by the way? Oh, I suppose it hardly matters. In any case, we can talk about Goldie later. I'm sure you'll see things my way, soon enough."

Not waiting for a response, Lady Keswick drifted away, leaving Margaret staring after her mother with a vague sense of foreboding.

Chapter Five

Margaret lay on her back in bed, staring up at the fabulously embroidered curtains looping above her head.

It was, without doubt, the largest and most comfortable bed she'd ever lain in. And yet, here she was, unable to sleep. Margaret bit back a sigh. It was full daylight outside, chinks of light squeezing their way in through gaps in the curtains. She couldn't delay getting up for much longer.

I'm a duchess today.

A knock at the door made her flinch, and she sat bolt upright, clutching the sheets around her shoulders.

"Who is it?" she quavered, feeling far more nervous than a brand-new duchess should.

"It is Mrs. Nettle, Your Grace," came a muffled woman's voice. "The housekeeper. I hope I have not woken you. I took the liberty of preparing a breakfast tray for you, and I thought I might introduce you to Isabel. May we come in?"

Margaret blinked, wondering whether she could say *no* at all. She decided that she probably could not.

"Of course, Mrs... Mrs. Nettle. Come in."

The door opened, and in strode a tall, confident-looking woman of middle age, with dark hair pulled back into a knot at the back of her head. She wore a plain grey stuff dress, and had her hands clasped coolly in front of herself.

A shorter, round-faced girl followed her, beaming with equal parts of excitement and anxiety, carrying a laden tray in her hands.

"I am Mrs. Nettle," the taller woman said, somewhat unnecessarily, "and this is Isabel. His Grace informed me that you would not be bringing your own maid, so I have taken the liberty of choosing Isabel to wait on you. She will do everything a lady's maid would do, and I must say that she is a sweet, biddable, and clever girl. I think you will like her. If you wish to get a maid of your own, Isabel will serve you well in the meantime."

Margaret blinked. It took a moment to collect herself, and she was uncomfortably aware that she was sprawled in bed, in her night gown, which did not exactly give her the upper hand in the conversation.

"Thank you," she managed at last. "That's very kind of you, Mrs. Nettle. I'm sure Isabel will suit me quite nicely. My breakfast looks delicious."

Were duchesses meant to give compliments like that? Not for the first time, Margaret was struck by how very ill-prepared she was for the role of a duchess.

Mrs. Nettle, however, gave her a small smile.

"Thank you, Your Grace. I was not sure what you would prefer for breakfast, so the Cook and I took the liberty of preparing a selection of things. I hope it meets with your expectations."

"I'm sure it shall."

Mrs. Nettle made a furtive gesture to Isabel, who crossed to the bed and carefully placed the table-tray across Margaret's knees. She stared down at the feast.

There was a plate of bacon, eggs cooked in several different ways, toast, bread, butter, mountains of jam, a whole kipper, some pastries, a small tureen of porridge with honey, and a bowl of fruit. And, of course, there was tea.

She swallowed hard.

"Enjoy your breakfast, Your Grace. Isabel and I will return shortly, and then I thought you might like a tour of the house?"

A tour. Of the house. Of *her* house. It occurred to Margaret then that she'd only seen a handful of rooms in the vast place. If she did not want to be embarrassingly lost in her own home, she had better learn her way around, and quickly.

"Yes, thank you," Margaret heard herself say. "I'd like that."

***

After breakfast, the business of dressing began. Isabel was good at her job, and quickly had Margaret stripped out of her night gown and into a fitted, fashionable green silk gown. She had no idea where the gown had come from, but there was a selection of unfamiliar dresses in the wardrobe, all in her size.

"His Grace had the gowns commissioned for you, Your Grace," Isabel said, following Margaret's gaze. "He remarked that you might desire some new gowns. We found it exceedingly gracious of him. We eagerly anticipate the presence of a true duchess among us, Miss M... I mean, Your Grace."

Margaret smiled weakly. "I'm not sure I feel like a *real duchess*, Isabel."

Isabel met her eye in the mirror, and there was sympathy there. "I imagine it takes time, Your Grace. Mrs. Nettle will help you, I'm sure. She's very serious, and a little strict, but the kindest, cleverest woman I have ever met."

"She has certainly been thoughtful," Margaret conceded, running a hand down the smooth silk of her bodice, marvelling at the quality of the material. "Do... do you know where the duke is this morning, Isabel?"

It was too embarrassing to admit that she had not seen him since their wedding.

Isabel frowned slightly. "I daresay he is presently attending to matters about the estates, Your Grace, in the company of Mr. Locke, the steward. The Stonehaven estate is indeed a grand and substantial property, as I am well aware. It requires considerable effort to manage such an enterprise. I am certain he shall join us for supper. There, you are all properly attired, Your Grace. Is there aught else you require?"

Margaret stared at her reflection. It felt odd, having another person flutter around her, helping her get dressed. Still, Isabel *had* done a good job. The dress was beautiful, and her hair was expertly done, twisted up on top of her head in carefully careless knots and twists, ringlets falling down over her neck.

"This is perfect, Isabel. Thank you."

Isabel beamed. "We should go then, Your Grace. Better not keep Mrs. Nettle waiting! She's excited to show you the manor, I know that much."

***

"... and here we have the Great Hall, which branches off into numerous chambers, each leading to further rooms and corridors," Mrs. Nettle elaborated. "The Great Hall extends nearly the entire length of the house. Should you find yourself disoriented, I advise you to focus on locating the Great Hall; it will serve as your guide. It is akin to an artery, coursing through the body."

"I think I will get lost, and very frequently," Margaret commented, feeling dazed. The house was *huge*, far larger than she'd expected. Mrs. Nettle had led her through room after room after *room*, casually mentioning a little something about each space they passed by.

"And this," Mrs. Nettle continued, turning to a huge, arched doorway, "is the library. Are you fond of books, Your Grace?"

Margaret beamed. "Oh, I am! How exciting!"

The library, like every other room they'd gone through, was huge. Vast, in fact. Bookshelves criss-crossed the walls, and there was a veritable maze of shelves in the centre of the room. A small balcony ran around the top of the room, and she could see yet more bookshelves up there. There were seats everywhere, of course. Smooth leather armchairs, velvety *chaise longues*, sprawling window seats. Dozens of places to curl up with a good book.

"I can't wait to browse the shelves," Margaret murmured.

"It *is* a remarkable collection," Mrs. Nettle acknowledged, sounding faintly proud. "The Stonehaven Library is one of the finest in the country. His Grace allows all of the household to borrow books whenever they choose, and only requests that they sign books in and out, in a ledger left near the door. However, as the Duchess, I imagine you will be exempt from that rule."

Margaret wandered towards the ledger in question, a hefty tome spread out on a low table, with a pencil beside it. Sure enough, there were neat rows of names, dates, and book titles spanning each page. She saw Mrs. Nettle's name, signed neatly as *J. Nettle*, alongside a few improving sorts of books. Isabel's name appeared a few times, next to novels, as well as many, many names she did not recognize at all.

"I don't mind signing out books with everybody else," Margaret said, throwing a smile over her shoulder. "I think it's a fabulous idea. But, Mrs. Nettle, I don't see his Grace's name here. Does he not care to read?"

Mrs. Nettle stiffened, almost imperceptibly.

"Oh, his Grace doesn't read much," Isabel piped up. "I never see him with a book."

Margaret chuckled. "A vast library like this, and he barely reads? What a waste! He *can* read, I assume?"

Perhaps it was a heavy-handed joke, but Margaret had not expected the icy, angry look that she caught from Mrs. Nettle. She blinked, flinching, and tried to work out where she had gone wrong.

"If that's all, Your Grace, I really must get back to my duties," Mrs. Nettle said coolly. "Supper will be at seven."

With that, she swept out, leaving Margaret bewildered and confused. Isabel, too, looked a little shocked.

What did I do? Margaret thought.

Chapter Six

Still puzzling over Mrs. Nettle's strange reaction to her joke earlier, Margaret approached the dining room. The day had slipped past faster than she might have expected, and while there'd been luncheon, of course, she found herself very ready for supper.

As she came closer, she could hear voices drifting out of the dining room. One was John Locke's, by the sound of it, and the other was quite clearly Jasper's. Her husband.

She stepped into the room, feeling as though she were intruding.

Sure enough, the two gentlemen were there, deep in conversation, and both turned to face her when she came in.

"Your Grace, it's a pleasure to see you again," John said, flashing a pained smile. "I..."

"John generally eats with me in the evenings," Jasper interrupted, barely glancing at Margaret. "Now he's saying that he can't eat with us anymore. I can't understand why not?"

John grimaced. "It's not *proper*, Jas... Your Grace. Your new wife would rather eat alone with you, I'm sure."

Margaret bit her lip. She knew, indeed, that some stewards were on good enough terms to sit down to meals with their employers, but it wasn't considered the *done thing*.

Jasper clearly did not understand this, and John seemed about to plunge into the ground from mortification.

"We're friends," Jasper said, sounding bewildered. "I can't understand why..."

"Of course John must join us," Margaret heard herself say. "See, the table is set for three. You *will* join us, won't you, Mr. Locke?"

John hesitated, only for a moment.

"Of course, Your Grace. Thank you."

Jasper gave a relieved smile, and the three of them settled down into their places. The duke sat at the head of the table at once, of course, and John automatically took a place at his right-hand side. That left the seat on the left for Margaret.

The table was a long one, stretching away to the other side of the room, easily big enough for twenty or thirty people, perhaps more. It felt strange, the three of them being cramped up at one end, dishes all around them.

But then again, what was the alternative? Spreading out, the three of them placed so far away from each other that they could barely see each other, let alone talk?

Margaret settled into her seat, placed her napkin on her lap, and let out a long, slow breath.

The first day of marriage is over. Only the rest of my life to get through.

A shiver rolled down her spine at that. She glanced at Jasper, leaning over his soup. He seemed entirely unaware of her existence, only directing the occasional comment towards John.

John was clearly uncomfortable.

I'm the guest, Margaret thought, with a dawning realization. *I am uninvited. There's no place for me.*

That was an upsetting thought. The food, while delicious, stuck in her throat. She glanced over at her new husband again, still all but oblivious to her presence.

He married me because dukes must *get married. Because paying off our debts and buying up our land will improve the Stonehaven estate. Because... oh, I don't know his reasons. For sure, though, he didn't marry me because of* me.

"Your Grace?"

She flinched at John's voice, dragging her gaze up from her plate.

"Hm?"

He tilted his head, looking a little anxious. "I said, are you settling in well, Your Grace?"

She smiled faintly. "I'm a little tired. That's all."

It was, of course, a lie.

***

A day passed, then two, then three. Margaret did not see her husband except for evenings, when the three of them sat down to supper together. John's anxiety seemed to lessen, once he realized that Margaret did not object to his presence. If anything, his presence made things easier. He was good at conversation and had easy manners and a jovial way about him that contrasted with Jasper's reticence.

No, not reticence, she was sure about that. It was sullenness.

As the days crawled by, Margaret's heart sank as she began to realize something disappointing.

Her new husband was avoiding her.

It was halfway through the afternoon of the fourth day after the wedding that things began to happen. Margaret found herself, as she often did, curled up on a seat in the library, reading in peace.

She heard the sound of hurrying footsteps from a distance, approaching the library. She had time to mark her place in her book and sit up by the time the footman burst in.

But it was not a footman, not the man she had been expecting. Mrs. Nettle stood there, an expression on her face which, on another woman, might have been interpreted as *worried*.

"There is a young woman here to see you, Your Grace," she said, an edge of anxiety in her voice. "Miss Marigold Molyneaux."

Margaret blinked. "*Goldie*? Goldie is here now?"

Mrs. Nettle nodded. "She has a suitcase with her, Your Grace. She is alone."

Something was wrong here, something terribly wrong.

Margaret set aside the book, rising to her feet.

"H-How did she…" she began, stammering.

"I believe Miss Molyneaux hired a coach," Mrs. Nettle responded. "The coach driver has not been paid, and the young lady admits to having no money with her. Do I have your permission to pay the coachman?"

"Of course, of course, Mrs. Nettle. Where is she now?"

"I put her in the parlour, and have sent for tea and cake. The girl looks shaken, Your Grace."

Margaret drew in a long, slow breath. "Thank you, Mrs. Nettle. And I think perhaps my sister may be staying with us earlier than we expected. If you could get her room ready, I would appreciate it."

Mrs. Nettle hesitated, just for a moment.

"I… I took the liberty of giving that order already, Your Grace. The room will be ready shortly."

Margaret had to smile at that. "Thank you, Mrs. Nettle. I appreciate it."

The housekeeper offered a brief curtsey and left the room. Heart thudding against her chest, Margaret scuttled away, not sure what scene awaited her in the parlour.

Goldie was crying.

She was huddled up in a ball on the sofa, her case abandoned on the floor beside her, knees drawn to her chest. Her hair was hastily pulled back, thick blonde strands escaping.

"Goldie?"

Her head shot up at the sound of her sister's voice, and Margaret saw that her face was tear-stained.

"Oh, Margaret!" she sobbed, hurtling up from the sofa and into her sister's arms. "Oh, Margaret, I missed you so much! It's been awful since you left. I know I shouldn't have come here, but I didn't know what to *do*, I didn't know where else to go!"

A flash of fear rolled through Margaret's chest. She swallowed hard, pulling back to get a good look at Goldie's tear-stained face.

"I'm always happy to see you. The coach has been paid, and your room will be all ready for you shortly. We'll have supper in an hour or two, and everything will be quite all right, I promise. I promise, do you hear me?"

Goldie nodded, gulping back tears. Margaret carefully tucked a loose curl of hair behind her sister's ear and steeled herself.

"Now, Goldie, I need you to tell me what has happened."

Goldie's face crumpled. "It's Mama. She was so strange after you left, and so very snappy. And then, only the next day, Lord Tumnus came to visit us. She'd invited him. It was just the three of us, and he hardly spoke to Mama at all. He kept sitting so close beside me and leaned entirely too close. I felt sick, Margaret, truly I did. He visited the next day, too, and I tried to pretend that I had a megrim and so couldn't see him, but Mama dragged me downstairs and made me talk to him. He was so unpleasant, and Mama just sat opposite on the sofa and did her sewing, and barely glanced up."

Goldie paused to suck in a deep breath, and Margaret tried to compose herself. Fury was building up inside her, hot and putrid, and she was obliged to take several deep, calming breaths before she spoke again.

"And what happened next?"

"I spoke to her about it today," Goldie sniffed. "I told her that I did not like Lord Tumnus and would not marry him under any circumstances. She said that young women did not understand things properly, and did not know how the world worked, and anyway I was not of age, so she would make such decisions for me and I should leave it up to her. I reminded her that you were married to the Duke of Stonehaven, and would take care of us, and she said that the Duke could not solve all of our problems but would not explain what she meant. And then I said that you had made her agree that I would not have to marry anyone I did not like, once you had married the duke."

"What did she say to that?"

Goldie sniffled. "She got terribly angry, Margaret. She shouted and railed and said that I was an unnatural, disobedient daughter, and you were a perverse wretch for making her promise such a thing, and anyway it was not binding in any way, and I would marry Lord Tumnus. Then she said… she said that he had already asked to marry me, and she had given him her permission. She said that it was all arranged, Margaret! She said that I was as good as engaged, and I ought to make my peace with it! I didn't know what to do, so I packed a few things and came straight here. I am sorry that I did not have money. The coach driver was very angry, but I told him that you would have money for sure, and when I told him you were the Duchess of Stonehaven, he brightened up considerably."

"The coachman is paid, dearest," Margaret consoled her sister. "Like I told you, everything is fine."

A little colour was returning to Goldie's cheeks now. She fished in her sleeve for a sodden handkerchief and blew her nose thoroughly.

"What about the duke?" she asked nervously. "Won't he be angry I'm here? Won't he say that I ought to marry Lord Tumnus?"

"No, he won't," Margaret said, as firmly as she could manage. "Now, let's get you up to your bedchamber. You need to wash your face and change your dress, it will make you feel better. Mrs. Nettle is going to rustle up some tea and cake, which will keep you going until suppertime."

Goldie brightened a little more at the prospect of tea and cake. "Are... are you sure you aren't angry at me?"

Margaret leaned forward, pressing a kiss to her sister's forehead.

"Never, Goldie. Never."

There was a tap on the door, and Mrs. Nettle entered.

"The guest bedroom is ready, Your Grace," she announced, smiling reassuringly at Goldie.

"Thank you, Mrs. Nettle. Could you take Goldie up to her room, please? And could she have her tea and cake there?"

"Of course. Come along, Miss Molyneaux," Mrs. Nettle extended her hand, and Goldie took it, smiling nervously at the taller woman. "What about you, Your Grace?"

Margaret drew in a deep breath. "I had better have a word with my husband. Tell me, Mrs. Nettle, where might I find him?"

Chapter Seven

Silence hung heavily over Jasper's study, broken only by the rhythmic scratch-scratch of his pen, and of John's, on the opposite side of the desk.

As always, John broke the silence first.

"I don't mind eating in the kitchen, Jasper, if you'd prefer to eat alone with the Duchess."

Jasper pursed his lips. "And why would I want to do that?"

John stared at him. "Because she is your wife. She is your wife, and you've barely spoken to her since you were married. Perhaps she's bored, or lonely."

"How can she be bored? There are endless things to do in a place like this. She can go wherever she wants, do whatever she wants. And she doesn't like me either, you know. She only married me to get her family out of debt. Mark my words, she is pleased that I leave her alone. I'd bet my fortune on it."

John sighed tiredly, putting down his pen and rubbing his eyes.

"I think perhaps that you do not understand women very well."

"And *you* do?"

"I think perhaps the Duchess would be open to friendship, at the very least."

Jasper clenched his jaw and said nothing. John did not understand. He had not been there for that humiliating meeting with the Molyneaux family. He'd seen greed flicker in Lady Keswick's eyes, seen the panic in the poor child's face — Marigold, that was her name — as her mother pushed her towards him.

He'd seen the determination in Margaret's face.

I should never have made her marry me.

The truth was, Margaret bothered him. He found himself thinking about her during the day, the way she'd looked at their daily dinner gatherings, things she'd said, things the servants had said about her. Mrs. Nettle was very taken by her, and if Janey Nettle liked a person, that was definitely a mark in their favour.

"Do you know what I think the trouble is here?" John said abruptly, leaning forward.

"I'm sure you're about to tell me."

"You like her. You're drawn to her. And it terrifies you."

He flinched, sitting back in his seat. "Do you know what I think?"

47

"Hm?"

"I think you ought to mind your own business, John."

Before John could respond, there was a tap at the door.

"Enter," Jasper called, assuming that it was Mrs. Nettle, or perhaps a footman, or...

The door opened, and Margaret stepped in. Immediately, there was silence in the room. John leapt respectfully to his feet at once, and Jasper was left sitting behind his desk, wondering if he were meant to get to his feet every time his duchess entered the room. He probably was.

Margaret was wearing a sprigged muslin gown, a simple white affair decked with blue ribbons. There was a sweet, florally scent about her which wafted into the room, cutting through the stale air of the study.

Jasper swallowed hard.

"Duchess. Er, Margaret. What brings you here?"

She hesitated for a moment, glancing at John. "I hoped we could talk in private. Mrs. Nettle told me you were here."

Well, if Mrs. Nettle sent her here, Jasper was fairly sure there was a good reason. He caught John's eye and gave him a brusque nod, a dismissal. John nodded back, collected his things, bowed to Margaret and then slipped away.

Once the door closed behind him, Margaret sucked in a breath and stepped forward, twisting her fingers together in front of her.

"My sister is here."

He lifted his eyebrows. "Miss Marigold?"

"Goldie, yes."

"I thought she wasn't due to arrive for another few weeks."

"She wasn't, but... but something has happened, and I think I will need your help."

He let out a slow breath, and gestured to the chair John had just vacated.

"Pray, take a seat. Kindly share your concerns, and I shall assist you to the best of my ability."

Relief filtered over her face. For some reason, it triggered a warm sensation in his chest, a feeling that Jasper was not used to feeling too often.

"You see, there is an older man that my mother thinks would make a good match for my sister. Lord Tumnus, perhaps you've heard of him?"

Jasper pursed his lips, tapping his fingers on the tabletop. "I have. It does not surprise me that he is pursuing your sister. His tastes run young. Too young."

"Yes, well, he's rich, and that's all Mama cares about these days. When I... when I agreed to marry you, I made Mama promise that Goldie could marry who she liked. I thought that was the end of it, but it seems I was wrong. Apparently, only the day after our wedding, she was inviting Lord Tumnus to the house, just the three of them. What's worse, he has apparently applied for her permission to marry Goldie, and she has accepted. Goldie isn't of age, and I worry... I worry that Mama might try to compel her into something. So, Goldie ran away and came here. I promised to protect her, but I don't know what to do next. Legally, can Mama come to take her back by force?"

He considered this, fingers tip-tapping on the desk. "I'm not sure. I would have to do research on the matter. You're right to keep your sister away from that man, by the way. Miss Marigold seems like a sweet girl, and with a half-decent dowry, I daresay she can have her pick of the *ton*. If she chooses to marry at all, that is. You will certainly be able to support her."

Margaret's shoulders seemed to relax a little more.

"She's just a child," she murmured. "I thought... I truly thought that Mama had listened to me. I don't understand. Why promise to leave Goldie alone if she intended to break her word all this time?"

Jasper considered. "Is that something your mother would do? Lie?"

Margaret flinched and there, Jasper supposed, was the answer. He leaned forward, resting his elbows on the desk.

"Look, Margaret. I have no intention of turning Miss Marigold back over to her mother, if that is what you're afraid of. She can stay here for as a long as she likes. She can make it her home, if she chooses, and I do mean that. I will speak to Lady Keswick, if you like. After all, if a good marriage is what she wants for her daughter, then surely you and I could facilitate that. The land and your home are bought up, so I can't imagine why she would be so keen to marry off the girl. Did she ever mention any other financial constraints to you?"

Margaret gave an unladylike snort. "I should say not. Mama never tells me anything. What is it about parents, do you think, that makes them simply *refuse* to trust their children? Is it because they perpetually see us as infants?"

Jasper bit his lip, conjuring up an image of a tall, severe man sneering down at him, at his *simple son*. He imagined a frail, weak woman in blue – always in blue – lounging on a couch, unable to stay awake for more than an hour at a time.

"I don't know," he found himself saying. "I just don't know."

Running footsteps sounded outside, and Jasper barely had time to straighten up in his chair before the door banged open. Mrs. Nettle stumbled in, out of breath.

She never runs, Jasper thought, with a flash of panic. *Something is wrong.*

"It is Lady Keswick," Mrs. Nettle panted.

"What about her?" he asked, biting the inside of his cheek.

"Well, she's *here*, Your Grace."

Chapter Eight

Jasper kept his head high as he strode down the passageway, aware of dozens of pairs of eyes on him. Margaret's, for one, scuttling at his side, lips pressed together in silent anxiety. There were Mrs. Nettle's eyes as well, more tired than she would care to admit.

Miss Marigold had come halfway down the stairs, the blood drained from her face, listening to the chaos at the front door. She watched Jasper in silence, tears streaking down her cheeks.

And, of course, plenty of the servants had hurried around to watch and listen.

In the days of the old duke, tempers ran high, and screaming matches and physical punishments were the norm. That hateful switch and cane he kept above his desk had been used, frequently, right up until Jasper got too big to be caned. He smiled grimly, remembering the day he had turned on his father and informed him that the old man could try and cane him, if he pleased, but then it would be Jasper's turn to try.

There had been no more attempts.

And there was no more shouting, either. The halls of Stonehaven Manor, which had once rung with angry bellows and screams, were peacefully quiet these days, seldom hearing even a raised voice.

The tinkling sound of shattering glass reached his ears. Glancing down at Margaret, he could see tension on her face. Without exchanging a word, they both began to walk a little faster.

The final stretch of hallway took Jasper to the foyer, directly in front of the large main door. The butler and a set of footmen were blocking Lady Keswick's entrance into the house. No doubt it was only Mrs. Nettle's impressive sixth sense for danger which had warned them that the woman ought not to be allowed entry.

As he approached, Lady Keswick picked up a delicate little chair – an antique – and threw it directly at a footman's head. The man ducked, and the chair flew over his head and shattered on the stone floor, bits of debris sliding almost to Jasper's feet.

Everybody glanced his way, and silence fell. Even Lady Keswick fell silent.

"Well," Jasper said at last, uneasily aware of all the eyes on him, "is anybody going to tell me what is going on here?"

"I am here to collect my daughter," Lady Keswick spoke up, at the exact same moment the butler said, "This lady demanded entry, even after we informed her that their Graces were not receiving guests. She forced her way inside and began to shout and throw things."

Margaret stepped forward, past Jasper. He was perfectly placed to see Lady Keswick's face change when she looked at her oldest daughter. He was a little shocked to see hatred there.

And perhaps more than a touch of jealousy.

"What *are* you doing, Mama?" Margaret hissed. "You just threw a chair. A chair! An antique, as a matter of fact. You nearly hit poor James. James, are you quite alright?"

"I am, thank you, Your Grace," the footman responded, and Margaret gave him a brief nod.

"Well, what have you to say for yourself, Mama? Did Goldie not leave a note?"

"No," Lady Keswick snapped. "She did not. Where is the ungrateful chit? I am taking her home at once."

"It is dark outside, Lady Keswick," Jasper spoke up. "I'm afraid I cannot countenance Miss Marigold going anywhere. If you were worried about her safety, you had only to write to me, or to Margaret, and you would have known at once that she was here, and quite safe."

Lady Keswick stared at him. The door behind her gaped open, letting periodical blasts of icy air into the house. Jasper shivered and glanced down to see shivers breaking out over Margaret's neck and bare forearms as well.

He hastily turned his gaze away.

"Do you understand the situation, Your Grace?" Lady Keswick asked nastily. "I imagine not. Whatever my daughter has told you..."

"Your daughter has told me enough. Come, we cannot have this conversation out in the open. Mrs. Nettle, would you please have tea sent to the parlour? The small one, nearest the door. It's comfortable enough and there should be a fire there at this time of day. I am sure Lady Keswick is willing to have a mature, genteel conversation about this matter."

There was a brief silence. Everybody glanced at Lady Keswick, whose face was blank and angry.

This is not a woman who likes to be humiliated, Jasper thought. *Well, I suppose that nobody does, not really, but she will take her revenge, if she considers herself wronged.*

"Very well," Lady Keswick said at last. "But I expect my other daughter to join."

Jasper hesitated, glancing over Mrs. Nettle. The housekeeper flashed a tight-lipped smile.

"Forgive me, Lady Keswick, but I believe that Miss Marigold is already in bed and asleep. You would not want to wake her, I'm sure."

Jasper bit back a smile at how easily the lie had tripped off his housekeeper's tongue. Lady Keswick looked angry, but did not say anything more.

It occurred to Jasper then that he should have looked at his *wife* for support in that matter, not his housekeeper. Too late now, though. Mrs. Nettle had been his friend, mother-figure, and confidante for many years, and he hoped that having a new lady of the house would not bother her too much.

"This way, Lady Keswick," Jasper said, when the silence grew too heavy. "Shall we?"

He extended a hand towards the direction of the small parlour. Should Lady Keswick be troublesome, it would be easier to get her out of the house. He hoped it wouldn't come to that. Manhandling one's mother-in-law out of the house only a few days after the wedding was certainly an inauspicious start.

He was wrong about the fire. The grate in the small parlour was bare, the chamber chill. A footman hastened to kindle a fire, yet it took some time for any whispers of warmth to pervade the room.

Lady Keswick took the largest, highest-backed armchair, sitting down as if mounting a throne. She kept her back straight, did not blink, and rested her wrists on the arms of the chair.

"You may sit," she said, as if the house was hers. "Margaret, why don't you start by telling me why you are keeping my daughter from me?"

Margaret stood where she was, fists clenched at her sides.

"You know why, Mama. You promised me Marigold would be safe, and now I hear that you're trying to force her into marriage with Lord Tumnus? She said that you agreed with him that he could marry her. You promised you would take care of her!"

Lady Keswick gave a slow, lazy blink, like an unimpressed cat.

"Is that what she told you?"

Jasper glanced between the two of them.

Margaret did not miss a beat. "Are you calling Goldie a liar, Mama?"

Lady Keswick heaved a sigh. She met Jasper's eye, eyebrows raising as if they were co-conspirators, laughing at a hidden joke over Margaret's head. He met her eye but kept his face smooth and blank.

"I am saying that Marigold is... is of a certain age. Girls of her age tend to be flighty, dramatic, prone to... well, prone to exaggerating. Lord Tumnus came to visit *me*, and of course Marigold was there. As to this business of an arranged marriage... well, I simply don't know where she would have gotten that idea. Too many novels, I imagine. I understand that forced marriages are a common theme in today's modern world." She paused, glancing over at Jasper. "You understand, don't you, Your Grace? Marigold is a harmless girl, but when they are at that age..." she paused, giving an expressive shrug. "One simply cannot believe a word they say."

"I'm sure some girls of that age *are* flighty, and over-imaginative, and even liars," Margaret responded. "But *Goldie* is not. She would not have run away from home, Mama, if she were not afraid of something."

"Perhaps. Let us bring her downstairs, then, and tell her that there is nothing to fear. I am her mother, Margaret, you cannot keep her from me."

Margaret was getting angry, Jasper could tell. Her face was turning redder and redder, and she kept glancing at Jasper as if for assistance. He knew that he *should* intervene, although he wasn't entirely sure what he was meant to say.

Perhaps Marigold *was* overreacting. Surely no mother would force a child of her age to marry a man like *Lord Tumnus*.

Even as he formed that hopeful thought, Jasper recalled his own parents, blank-faced and disinterested, sometimes armed with a slipper, switch, or cane, ready to discipline any unwanted behaviour. Mistakes were not allowed.

It would be better to believe Marigold for now, he decided, and risk upsetting Lady Keswick for a while.

"May I make a suggestion?" he spoke up. The two women, whose voices were raising higher and higher, both paused mid-sentence and turned to look at him. He cleared his throat, adjusting his cuffs.

"Miss Marigold was meant to stay with Margaret and me anyway, wasn't she? What is the harm in having her arrive a little earlier? She is here now, so she might as well stay."

Lady Keswick missed a beat. "But... your honeymoon, Your Grace."

He barely managed to bite back a bitter smile. *Honeymoon? What honeymoon? We've avoided each other studiously since the day we were married. I even insisted on John continuing to join us for meals, so that she wouldn't have to be alone with me.*

"I don't mind Marigold staying here. As I said, she's already here."

Lady Keswick mustered up a tight smile. "But her come-out..."

"I will bring her out into Society," Jasper said, a little shocked at the words coming out of his own mouth. "Well, Margaret and I shall bring her out. I can host decent parties here, and Margaret can chaperone her sister. It would work nicely, don't you think?"

There was a long pause after this. He was vaguely aware of Margaret staring at him, but kept his gaze on Lady Keswick.

"And where is my place in all of this?" Lady Keswick asked at last, voice sweet. "I, her mother?"

"You can stay here if you like," Jasper said, once again ignoring the intense stare from his wife. "There's plenty of room. It might be a *little* uncomfortable for you, as Margaret now outranks you, but I'm sure that doesn't matter at all to such a devoted mother. You can even invite guests of your own here. Although not, of course, Lord Tumnus."

There was an even longer pause after this. Jasper felt the urge to fidget, to cross and re-cross his legs, or fiddle with his cuffs, or to even clear his throat and fill the silence with some more words. He forced himself to stay still, however, and waited for Lady Keswick to reply.

"Well," she said at last, voice tart. "How very kind of you. I'm afraid I'm not ready to give up my independence just yet. My oldest daughter, regardless of what she might have told you, is not willing to share a home with me, I think."

Margaret flushed. "Mama, how could you say that? I only do this to protect Goldie. You *know* how I always took care of her."

"Hm, yes. If you had your way, she'd die a spinster."

"If that is what Goldie wants for her life, then yes, I would support her in such a matter."

Lady Keswick gave a bark of mirthless laughter and rose to her feet. "Very well. I can see that I've worn out my welcome, so I shall take my leave. I apologise for the chair, by the way."

Jasper bit his lip. "Think no more of it. I'll call a carriage for you, and..." he trailed off when Lady Keswick fixed him with a ferocious stare.

"Thank you, Your Grace, but I am entirely capable of bringing my own carriage. Good night to you both."

She sailed out of the room, head held high, never once looking back.

There was a gaggle of servants outside. Not eavesdropping but clearing up the mess Lady Keswick had made. There were muddy footsteps trailing in front outside, which a maid was diligently mopping, and the splinters from the broken chair were being swept up by a footman. The butler oversaw them all, and a maid was on her knees picking up shards of glass, presumably from the glass vase Jasper had heard shattering earlier.

They all glanced around when the door opened and stared at Lady Keswick standing there. The silence was heavy.

Lady Keswick seemed unperturbed, and simply strode towards the door.

"I shall visit you tomorrow, Mama," Margaret called suddenly. "We'll talk about this."

Lady Keswick did not stop, or turn around, or acknowledge at all that she had heard a word of what her daughter had said. She threw open the door and disappeared down the steps and into the growing darkness.

The silence she'd left behind her seemed to grow tighter by the minute. Jasper cleared his throat, simply to get some *sound* into the atmosphere.

The butler edged forward, looking awkward.

"My apologies for not having this tidied up sooner, Your Graces. We thought that we had more time. It will be cleaned up directly."

He shook his head vaguely. "Don't worry about it, truly. If Lady Keswick arrives at the house again, either me or her Grace, the Duchess, is to be consulted before she is let in."

The butler swallowed. "Yes, Your Grace."

Jasper felt a faint tug at his sleeve, and glanced down to find Margaret's fingers pinching at the fabric. She was staring up at him, an odd expression on her face.

"Did you really mean what you said? About us taking Goldie into Society?"

He cleared his throat. "I suppose we'd better."

"Even after... I mean, forgive me, but I thought that you hated Society."

He stared down at her for a long moment. She began to blush, and it occurred to him that it probably seemed as if he were glaring at her, angrily, instead of simply being lost in thought. To counteract the effect, he tried for a jovial smile. It probably came out looking like a pained sneer, but it was too late now.

"I do hate Society," he responded simply. "Do excuse me, Margaret. I had better change for supper."

With that, he hurried away from her, heading towards the staircase.

Why is my heart beating so fast? What is wrong with me? What has she done to me? And more to the point, how *has she done it?*

Chapter Nine

"How did you sleep?" Margaret asked, letting herself into the guest room. It was their nicest one, large and plush and recently cleaned and aired. It always seemed unfair to Margaret to put the youngest guests in the worst rooms, the way her mother had told her that things were meant to be done. It was *unfair*. Besides, Goldie had had a nasty shock, and deserved a nice bed.

Goldie yawned and stretched, arms reaching above her head. Tangled up in the pillows and blankets as she was, she seemed even smaller and younger than usual.

"I slept very well, considering. I had nightmares about Lord Tumnus crawling in the window and taking me away, though. Mama was right there, sitting in *that* chair," she pointed at a little armchair set beside the fire, "and only smiled and smiled, doing her sewing, and didn't do anything to help me."

Margaret felt a pang. "That's awful, darling. Well, no need to worry, as I shan't let Lord Tumnus come near you."

Goldie bit her lower lip. "Or Mama?"

"Well, she is our mother, so we'll have to see her sometime. But the duke told her that you would stay here, and we would take you into Society."

Goldie brightened. "Do you mean parties and balls and such?"

"Indeed, things like that."

The excitement gradually drained from her face. "I don't like them so much, though, because I always have to be looking for a husband while I'm there. I don't want a husband."

Margaret hesitated for a moment, setting down the breakfast tray. She had begged Mrs. Nettle to let her take up the tray, so that she and Goldie could eat breakfast together. Mrs. Nettle was faintly scandalized at the idea of a duchess carrying up a breakfast tray – and not even her own! – but eventually gave in to Margaret's pleading.

Once the breakfast tray was in place, Margaret settled herself onto the bed, propped up by pillows beside her sister, and helped herself to a strawberry.

"Do you not want to get married at all, Goldie?"

Goldie thought it over for a long moment, her brow furrowed.

"I... I don't know. Lots of girls my age talk all the time about getting married. About beaus, and weddings, and children. They seem so excited for all of that, and I suppose I'm just... I'm just not. I always expected to get married. Mama said that I would marry a rich man and save us all. But then, I suppose, *you* have married the rich man. Oh, is he nice to you, Margaret?"

Margaret chuckled. "Will you murder him if I say no?"

"I might, but I think he's kind enough. He was pleasant to me, at least."

"Well, I can assure you that he's a very kind man, and mostly leaves me alone. We avoid each other, I think."

Goldie frowned again. "Oh. That's rather sad."

"If you say so. But, Goldie, do you truly not want to get married? Not ever?"

"Perhaps one day I would like to marry, if I met somebody I *wanted* to marry. But..." she swallowed, picking at the covers. "Not yet. I don't want to get married yet, Margaret. I told Mama that, and she was ever so angry."

Margaret reached out, taking Goldie's hand and squeezing it.

"You don't have to get married if you don't want to, Goldie," she said quietly. "I can promise you that."

Marigold smiled faintly, but Margaret had a sneaking feeling that her sister did not believe her.

***

Margaret fidgeted inside the unfamiliar carriage, trying to calm her nerves. It wasn't as though the carriage was uncomfortable – quite the reverse, in fact. It belonged to Jasper, of course, and had the family crest emblazoned on the side. People turned and stared as the vehicle rumbled grandly down the streets, and Margaret felt inclined to wilt back into her seat, and maybe pull the curtains across.

She did no such thing, of course. By the time her courage waned and she began to think that she was being silly, it was too late, and they were there.

The carriage halted, and Margaret found herself staring up at her old home.

I've only been gone for five days, she thought to herself, *yet the place already feels so alien to me. How strange.*

There was no sense in allowing herself to fidget and worry inside, though, and Margaret forced herself to climb out of the carriage.

As her feet hit the pavement, however, the door opened, and a familiar figure came out, forcing a hat on his head as he went. He twirled a cane in one hand, and his face was screwed up in an expression of distaste.

He barely glanced at her, and would have gone striding right by if Margaret hadn't spoken.

"Lord Tumnus," she said. "What a surprise to see you here."

He paused, glancing up at her as if seeing her for the first time. As before, his gaze skipped over her face as if she were too plain for him to even look at – or, more likely, too old – but the fur cape she wore and the expensive, yellow gauze gown made him look twice.

"Miss Molyneaux," he said, with visible reluctance. "Except, it isn't Miss Molyneaux anymore, is it?"

She allowed herself an unladylike grin, showing teeth.

"No, it isn't. You may call me *Your Grace*, by the way."

He didn't like that. Lord Tumnus bridled, looking as though he would like to storm away.

Before he could make his escape, Margaret took a step forward. He retreated backwards, which was gratifying.

"Before you go, I should like to say something to you, Lord Tumnus."

"Well, go on, then," he snapped, in a distinctly ungentlemanly fashion. "What is it?"

"Any understanding you may think you have with my sister, Miss Marigold, is, I'm afraid, entirely at an end. You will have found out, by now, that she is no longer living with our mother here. Marigold is under my protection, and I suggest you forget any hopes you might have had of her. I am sorry for your disappointment, but you are not the man for my sister. Not at all."

He was silent for a moment, not immediately responding.

"I am not sure you are the one to make that decision, madam," he said, speaking slowly. He deliberately left off her title, she noticed.

"No, Marigold is the one to decide. And she has no interest in you, Lord Tumnus. None at all."

He sneered. "You, my dear, are simply jealous."

Margaret couldn't help it. She let out a titter of laughter, loud in the quiet street. Lord Tumnus reddened with anger.

"I am sorry," she managed at last, a gloved hand over her mouth. "I must respectfully submit that your assertion is not entirely accurate. I trust there are no lingering grievances between us, yet I felt it my duty to express myself with utmost clarity."

"You were clear," he snarled, pushing his hat further down on his head. "Crystal clear, my dear."

With that, he turned on his heel and stamped away.

Margaret watched him go. It seemed so unfair for a man to get away with all sorts of cruelties and vices, simply because he had money. With a shudder, Margaret realized just how lucky she had been to marry Jasper, who had money and power and – most importantly of all – the *inclination* to help. Goldie was safe, and if she could remain safe, then marrying Jasper had been worth it.

Not that Jasper had been unkind to her in any way. If anything, he'd been rather solicitous towards her. He was brusque, to be certain, but... oh, she didn't know. Margaret found herself thinking of him frequently. Ordinarily, a woman thinking of her husband regularly would only be natural, but in her case, how natural could it be? She hardly knew anything about the man, beyond what light, stilted conversation could be exchanged over a dinner table.

Sighing, Margaret climbed the steps and knocked on the door. Part of her expected not to be let in, but the door was opened and she was ushered into their familiar little parlour.

Lady Keswick sat in her usual seat, face impassive. She didn't offer Margaret a seat, but Margaret sat anyway.

"I didn't think you'd come," Lady Keswick said at last.

"I didn't think you'd let me in," she responded. "I see Lord Tumnus was here."

Lady Keswick scowled. "Of course. He's a decent man, you know."

"Then why don't you marry him, Mama?"

"Don't be ridiculous. Even if I had an inclination to marry again, I am far too old for him."

"You and he are fairly close in age. Closer, I should think, than Goldie and him."

Lady Keswick heaved an impatient sigh. "I am thoroughly sick of you, Margaret. Lord Tumnus is a decent man."

"I think we both know that he is not. I warned him off, by the way. We shan't let him near Goldie again."

There was a long, taut silence, during which the two women stared at each other. It would have been up to Lady Keswick to ring for tea, which she did not do. It was a breach of etiquette, of course, but no more than Margaret had expected.

"You do your sister no favours, you know," Lady Keswick said at last. "Marigold has strange ideas. She wants to study odd subjects and waste her youth withering away in libraries. She thinks that life can be about something other than sacrifice and disappointment. I remember thinking that way, and I wish somebody had knocked those ideas out of my head before they had the chance to take root."

Margaret pressed her lips together. "Studying odd subjects, you say? Do you mean Latin, and Arithmetic? Geography and geometry and literature? Botany? History? You think they are *odd subjects* to study?"

"For a woman, yes," Lady Keswick retorted at once. "Women and men live different lives, Margaret. Don't be obtuse. You know this."

Margaret took her time in replying. She leaned back in her seat, glancing around the room. How small and shabby it looked now. How cold, and uninviting with her mother looming in the corner.

At home already she was thinking of Stonehaven Manor as *home* Margaret had a private parlour. It was a small room, deliberately chosen for its cozy atmosphere, and well-furnished. She had a bookshelf in it, various pieces of furniture and a few ornaments from around the house that she'd found interesting, and so on. It was hers. *Hers.*

"I spoke to Goldie, after you left yesterday," Margaret said at last.

"Oh? Not in bed, then, was she?"

"You drove her to it, Mama. You try and convince me otherwise, but I know you, and I know Goldie. I believe that you were trying to force her into an engagement with Lord Tumnus."

Something like guilt passed across Lady Keswick's face. It was only there for a moment, then she was back to her usual, stony self. She lifted her chin high, meeting Margaret's eye defiantly.

"Well, and what if I were? I do not assert that I was endeavouring to arrange an engagement, mind you. However, were I to do so, I would be fulfilling my duty as a mother. Lord Tumnus is of commendable lineage, a gentleman of means, and possesses a most respectable character."

"Respectable! Ha!"

"He is willing to marry Marigold, who has nothing," Lady Keswick continued, as if Margaret had not spoken. "Any decent mother would agree. Marigold is a silly little girl with foolish ideas about love and independence. She needs marriage to settle her down. I am her mother, and therefore I know what is best for her."

"Those two things do not necessarily go hand in hand. And if Marigold is so silly and short-sighted when it comes to the future, ought we to be marrying her off so soon? Should she not grow up a little, and experience the world?"

Abruptly, Lady Keswick leaned forward, eyes narrowed. "We are women, Margaret. We do not *experience the world*. The only thing growing women do is march down the altar to become wives, and then lie on a birthing bed to become mothers. There is nothing else for us in this life, I'm afraid, nothing at all."

Margaret shook her head vigorously. "I can't believe that."

"Then you are as delusional as she is. Are you here to return my daughter, Margaret, or not?"

"Not."

Lady Keswick rose to her feet. "Then I suppose you should leave. We have nothing to say to each other."

Margaret flushed, a little taken aback.

"Pray, is this what it has come to? You are casting me out?"

Lady Keswick pursed her lips. "You almost threw me out of your home, did you not?"

"I have spoken to Goldie, Mama. She does not *want* to marry Lord Tumnus. Or anyone, just yet!"

"She doesn't understand," Lady Keswick responded stubbornly. "Neither of you do. I should be making the decision, as your mother. I should not have brokered that marriage between the duke and you, Margaret. It was a mistake."

Margaret bit back a sigh. "Mama, Jasper is going to take Goldie into Society. He might even give her a dowry."

"Men cannot be relied on, my dear," Lady Keswick murmured, hand darting out as though she were going to touch Margaret's cheek. "He promises all sorts of things, but just wait and see if he follows through."

She flinched at that. Surely that couldn't be true, could it? Some men – most, perhaps – were unreliable, but surely not all?

"If men are so unreliable," she found herself saying, "why are you so keen for Goldie to marry one of the worst?"

Lady Keswick's hand dropped, and her face set into a scowl.

"There is no sense in reasoning with you. Are you going to return my daughter or must I approach a magistrate?"

Margaret bit back a sigh of disappointment. For a moment, just a moment, it had really felt as though she and her mother were getting somewhere.

An illusion, of course. Lady Keswick was stubborn, painfully so, and had never admitted to a thing she did not truly agree with. Margaret had no doubt that her mother would never, never admit that Lord Tumnus was the worst possible choice for Goldie.

"No, Mama," she heard herself say, voice quiet. "And I'm not sure a magistrate would return her, not when she doesn't want to go. Not when she's safe with Jasper and me. He is the Duke of Stonehaven, after all."

Lady Keswick smiled nastily. "I certainly hope he doesn't get tired of Marigold. And tired of you. Men are so changeable."

"But I am not changeable, Mama," Margaret snapped, a sudden rush of anger swelling up inside her. "And I will not let you push Goldie in danger. Do you hear me? I will not."

She didn't wait for an answer. Turning on her heel, Margaret stormed out, out to the waiting carriage. She didn't turn around, knowing full well that her mother was staring at her from the parlour window.

Margaret climbed into the carriage and thumped on the roof.

"I am ready," she said shortly, and promptly burst into tears.

Chapter Ten

Margaret's tears had mostly dried up by the time she reached home. Which was just as well, since Goldie was waiting anxiously for her at the front steps.

"Well?" she said, as Margaret climbed down from carriage. "How did it go? How was Mama?"

"Well enough," Margaret said, as vaguely as possible. She was aware of the footmen lingering by the door, no doubt hearing every word. "Let's talk in the parlour."

Apparently, she was not convincing enough. Goldie's face fell. The younger girl swallowed, anxiety filtering into her expression.

"I asked for them to bring tea there," she said, a little flatly. "It did not go well, did it?"

Margaret let out a long exhale, shoulders sagging. "No," she confessed. "No, it did not."

They sat for a few long moments in the parlour, while Mrs. Nettle herself set out the tea service.

"Thank you," Margaret said, once the process was complete. "I wonder, Mrs. Nettle, if you could tell his Grace that I wish to speak to him later? Is he in his study?"

Mrs. Nettle did not betray any surprise. "No, Your Grace, he is not. I am not sure where he is, only that he is out and about with his steward. He may not return until dinner time. I could try and find out for you, if you like."

Margaret swallowed, nodding. "Yes, I think that would be best. If you can, of course."

Mrs. Nettle gracefully inclined her head and left without another word. The silence stretched out even longer.

"Mama isn't going to let me stay here, is she?" Goldie said, flatly. "I should have known it. She's going to create trouble, isn't she?"

Margaret considered telling, if not a straight lie, something a little more palatable than the truth.

She decided against it. Their mother had a habit of stretching and sweetening the truth when it suited her, and it had never made *her* seem more trustworthy, or made the eventual reveal of the truth any easier to grasp.

"I'm not sure," Margaret managed at last. "There was talk of magistrates."

Goldie groaned aloud, setting down her teacup with a clatter. "Oh, oh, no! Well, that's that, I suppose. I can't let her hurt you."

"She won't *hurt* me. She can't."

"But the magistrate…"

"She only *talked* about the magistrates. There's a chance she might decide to leave it."

"She won't," Goldie murmured, staring despondently at her feet. "I don't know when it begun, this obsession with me marrying a rich man. I really did think that once you married the Duke, she would leave me alone, but she hasn't abated her determination, not one bit. I do not understand."

"There's something she isn't telling us, for certain," Margaret said firmly, taking a sip of her tea. It was too hot, and scalded her tongue. "But that's not the point here. The point is, Goldie, you are *not* going back to her, and you are not marrying Lord Tumnus. Mama made an agreement to let you stay, and I won't let her go back on it."

"But the magistrates…"

"It could only be a threat. I will take care of this, Goldie, I promise."

Margaret reached out, taking her sister's hand. Goldie's hand was limp and cold, and she did not return Margaret's reassuring squeeze.

"But what if you can't?" Goldie mumbled, half speaking to herself. "Mama is far cleverer than either of us, and she invariably secures her own desires on all other occasions. Why should this instance be any different?"

"It doesn't matter. I will take care of *you*, Goldie."

"What magistrate would let you keep me, over our mother's right to raise me?"

Margaret drew in a breath. "It's not my right we'll be asserting. It will be the duke's."

Goldie glanced up at her. "You truly think that a magistrate would favour the duke – who is not even a blood relative – over Mama?"

She swallowed hard. It was a painful truth, but one she could not swerve away from.

"Yes. Indeed, I think he might. The duke is a man, after all, and a powerful one. A rich one, too. That might work in our favour."

It was clear that Goldie was not reassured. She nibbled her lower lip, mulling it all over in her mind.

"I hope it does," she said at last. "Because I'm not sure I have the strength to stand up to Mama anymore. If I were to return to her, I daresay I would find myself wed to Lord Tumnus. I am certain of it. She would insist upon it and I am not... not like you, Margaret. I lack fortitude. I am not strong enough."

Margaret flinched and had to look away from the bleak despondency on her sister's face.

"It won't come to that," she said shortly. "I promise you that."

Goldie tried valiantly to smile, and Margaret could almost hear the unspoken words.

I wish I could believe you.

***

"I have it on good authority he is just across the way, by that ridge you can see from the window," Mrs. Nettle said, pointing. "It's the border of some farmland which pushes up against our land. A tenant farmer rents from us, and his Grace has been discussing some matters with him. If you go now, you're likely to meet him."

"Thank you," Margaret said, breathing out. She had rejected the idea of getting a horse saddled up for her or sending a footman to carry a message. This was an important conversation that must be had, and it ought to be had face-to-face. Sending a crisp message to summon her husband to the house like an errand boy did not seem like a good start.

"Forgive me, Your Grace," Mrs. Nettle began, just as Margaret was about to put a foot out of doors, "it's not my place to speak, but I had to say something."

"Oh?"

"It is clear that you are having trouble with Miss Marigold – who, I must say, is a fine young woman and much liked below-stairs. If you require any help or advice, I would be happy to help in any way I can. I am an older woman than you, Your Grace, and have seen a little more of life. My experience may come in handy."

She folded her hands neatly across her middle and waited patiently for Margaret to respond.

For some reason, it felt like a test.

Margaret bit the inside of her cheek, thinking. "I have a rather sensitive matter to discuss with his Grace. A personal one. I... I don't wish to be demanding, or to offend him, but it's also crucial I get his help in this matter. You know him well. How should I approach him?"

There was an imperceptible softening in the lines around Mrs. Nettle's mouth, and Margaret got the sense of having passed the test.

"Simply be yourself, Your Grace," Mrs. Nettle said, after a pause. "Be frank. Do not lie to him, or distort the facts, no matter how bare and unappealing they may be. He reacts poorly if he believes he has been lied to in any way. And trust to his goodness. Despite his brusque manner, he is a good man and a fair one, and more generous than you can believe."

Margaret swallowed, nodding. "I see. Thank you, Mrs. Nettle. This was helpful."

The older woman inclined her head and said nothing. When Margaret hurried out of the doorway, Mrs. Nettle stayed behind, standing in the doorway and watching her go.

The ground was wet, shifting and sticking under Margaret's boots. Every step was an effort, and she nearly lost her balance more than once.

That would ruin everything, of course. Margaret hoped to appear like a *proper* duchess, composed and cool and ready to have a genteel conversation with her husband. The effect would be utterly spoiled if she were to appear, clumsily stumbling into view, her gown soiled and tattered, her hair hanging in disheveled wisps about her countenance, utterly beyond salvage.

No, this was a serious conversation. If the duke declined to help Goldie stay free of Lady Keswick, that was that. Margaret knew full well that as an older sister – even a duchess – she did not have any right to keep Goldie from her legal guardian. She wasn't even sure that the duke had such a right. If he would not help her, it was all over.

Really, she should have waited till he came home, and had their conversation in his study, where he would feel at ease and in control.

My own impatience is going to be the death of me, Margaret thought sourly, struggling to climb over a stile.

She was still navigating the stile, her skirts seeming determined to cling onto the fence, and otherwise trip her and send her tumbling into a muddy puddle waiting for her at the bottom of the stile.

Am I... am I stuck?

A distant shout caught her attention. Margaret glanced up, spotting a trio of men silhouetted against the sky, further up at the peak of the hill.

Wonderful. An audience.

There was a muffled exchange between the men, and then one began to jog down the hill towards her. He moved swiftly and easily, sure-footed on the shifting mud. About halfway down the hill, Margaret realised with a sinking heart that the man was, of course, her husband.

She was tempted to try and jump down and go to meet him, but any movement would almost certainly send her plunging down into the mud. She was forced to stand and wait.

"May I offer my assistance?" Jasper shouted, when he was close enough.

Margaret's pride wanted to say *no, thank you, I am quite all right,* but that would be an obvious lie.

"Yes, if you please," she admitted. "This stile is proving more difficult than I expected."

"It's a narrow one, sure enough," Jasper acknowledged. "Allow me! I shall help you down."

He reached up with both arms, and before Margaret could realize that he was not simply offering her a helping hand, he grasped her around the waist and lifted her bodily down from the stile.

There was an odd sensation of weightlessness – the man was certainly much stronger than Margaret had expected – and then her feet touched solid ground.

Well, solid-ish.

"Th-Thank you," she stammered, feeling oddly breathless for some reason. "I feel like such a fool."

Jasper only grunted. "You've chosen an odd place for a walk. This field is nothing more than churned-up mire, and the field is used by the tenant farmer who manages it. Are you sure you wouldn't prefer a walk with a proper path?"

She cleared her throat. "Actually, I was looking for you."

Something flickered over his face, hastily concealed.

"I see," he said at last. "And it couldn't wait until tonight?"

"I... I don't believe so. It's rather urgent, and I wanted to speak to you at once. I'm sorry, mayhap this was a bad idea. Mrs. Nettle said you were busy."

"Janey sent you out here? Well, it must be important, then. Pray, do enlighten me."

Margaret blinked at the casual use of the childish nickname. She couldn't imagine the severe, stolid Mrs. Nettle being called *Janey* by anyone.

But now wasn't the time for that, not with Jasper looking down at her with that quietly serious expression on his face, waiting patiently for her to explain.

So she launched into the story – her visit to her mother's home, Lady Keswick's barely-veiled threats, the mention of magistrates. Jasper's expression grew darker and darker, and he did not interrupt or speak a word until he was quite sure that she was finished.

"Well, this is a difficult situation," he said at last. "Your mother agreed that Marigold could stay here, did she not?"

"Yes, but she's gone back on her word. She wants Marigold to marry that man. Lord Tumnus."

"I'm familiar with him. Do you think she really will go to the magistrate?"

Margaret covered her face with her hands. "I don't know. I don't *know*. My mother has always been difficult, but this is... this is something quite different. I don't understand why she is suddenly acting this way. I am afraid... that is, I think that perhaps something is going on. Something Mama is not telling me about."

Jasper folded his arms across his broad chest. Lost in thought, he scowled to himself.

"I cannot understand a parent's perverse desire to see their children miserable, at any rate."

Margaret flinched. "I... I wouldn't have said that Mama *wants* to see Goldie miserable or even me."

"Are you sure? Because forcing one's child into a marriage is, in my opinion, a true failure of parenting. My own parents could not have been less concerned for my well-being, save for their desire to ensure the continuation of their lineage. My father always said..."

Jasper broke off abruptly, reddening. He bit his lip, looking away, and Margaret got the sense that he felt he had said too much. She had certainly never heard him speak so frankly about his childhood. He had not really given anything away, beyond the miserable fact that his parents were not good parents at all, not one bit.

"I... I believe I have upset you," she stammered. "I would not have bothered you with all of this, only that if I am to keep Goldie here with me, I believe I will need your support. If my mother does choose to go to the magistrates and so on, I mean."

He nodded. "You were wise to speak to me about this. The trouble is, Lady Keswick could scoop Marigold up from the streets and drag her bodily home and would be well within her rights to do so. A fair magistrate might acknowledge that while Marigold is not of age, she *is* old enough to know her own mind and take that into account. A worse magistrate might simply ignore her wishes and send her back to her legal guardian," he paused, pinching his chin. "But if *I* were applying for guardianship of her..."

"But you are not a blood relative."

"No, I am not, but the law consistently favours the rights of man above the rights of woman, especially in matters of child custody. For example, a wife who leaves even the worst of husbands is obliged to leave her children behind. It is not particularly fair, but in this instance, it might benefit us. I would need to do some research into the matter, though."

Margaret brightened. "You'll help me?"

He glanced at her properly, and she could have sworn that he reddened slightly, before he turned his back.

"Of course," he answered shortly. "I shall speak to Lady Keswick myself, if I can, and investigate the matter. Perhaps there's some precedent here."

It was as if a weight lifted from Margaret's shoulder. She wanted to grin and laugh. The problem was not solved, of course. Not by a long shot, but Jasper was going to *help* her.

"Oh, I'm so glad! We can research together, and..."

"No," he interrupted sharply, making her flinch. "No," he repeated, a little more mildly. "No, I must be allowed to pursue this myself. Do you understand?"

"Y-Yes," she managed, feeling ill-at-ease.

He gave a short nod. "Splendid."

With that, he turned on his heel and began to stride back up the hill again, leaving Margaret to navigate her way back over the stile by herself.

Chapter Eleven

Jasper turned the matter over and over in his head, analysing it from every angle.

On the one hand, he disliked the idea of using his advantage as a man and a duke to force a mother away from her child, but he had seen the look in Lady Keswick's eyes the last time they met. He'd seen the fear in Marigold's eyes, too.

But what now?

He longed to talk the matter over with John, but he was busy sorting out the matter of the tenant farmer, who needed some repairs done to his farmhouse and elsewhere on the land. A simple enough matter, and one that John could easily manage himself. So, there was no reason for Jasper to stay out on the land.

It was a cold day, the wind high and blustery, and Jasper walked fast, head down. Thinking, always thinking.

Mrs. Nettle greeted him at the door. She didn't give him any extra information, or anything he might have missed. He trusted that there was nothing he needed to hear, then. Janey had always been loyal to him. They had too much shared history to ever consider parting, and he trusted her more than any other living person.

"How is Miss Marigold settling in?" he asked, as she helped him out of his heavy, grubby work-coat."

"Not well," Mrs. Nettle responded with a sigh. "The girl is on edge, and remarkably timid. I believe she does not dare let herself feel at home. The servants all like her, however. Myself included."

"We both know that you are barely a servant, Janey."

Mrs. Nettle chuckled. "Always so generous. I take it that her Grace talked to you about the current problem?"

"She did. Have you any advice?"

Mrs. Nettle paused, considering. A line appeared between her brows as she thought.

"Don't underestimate Lady Keswick," she said at last. "Never underestimate a woman with everything to lose. She is desperate, and I cannot work out why."

Jasper pursed his lips, unable to shake a feeling of unease. "I'm sure it will reveal itself in time. Where is Miss Marigold?"

"The music room, I believe."

***

Jasper heard music filtering out of the room long before he approached it. The room hadn't been used for years – for a decade, perhaps – and no doubt it was dusty and neglected. He winced, wishing he'd asked Mrs. Nettle to embellish the room. Too late now, of course.

He hesitated in the door, which stood ajar a little.

Marigold sat at the pianoforte, rapt. The melody was a simple one, and a very old one. He guessed that she'd taken sheet music from where it was stored beside the piano and had not brought any of her own music. There were more modern pieces that Society enjoyed, music which changed with the fashion of the Season.

Marigold finished playing with a flourish and a sigh. Movement attracted his notice, and Jasper noticed for the first time that Margaret sat on a *chaise longue* facing the pianoforte and listening to her sister carefully. She clapped her hands.

"Well done, Goldie! You have a real talent, you know."

Marigold blushed, smiling. "Oh, I don't know. Some other ladies can play so much better than…" she glanced up, catching sight of Jasper in the doorway, and the colour drained from her face. Bouncing to her feet, she directed her eyes at the floor. "Your Grace! I didn't know you were there."

Just like that, the atmosphere in the room changed. Margaret got to her feet too, eyeing him carefully. Jasper tried not to feel hurt at the way their smiles had vanished.

"I'm sorry to interrupt," he said.

"Mrs. Nettle said I could play the pianoforte here," Marigold burst out, shifting nervously. "I did not think…"

"Of course, you can," he interrupted. "Play the pianoforte here whenever you like. There is a harp somewhere, and a fiddle or two, and a guitar, and all sorts of instruments and sheet music. This was my mother's room, and I daresay hasn't been used for ten years or more. Consider it yours, Marigold. And you too, Margaret."

Marigold brightened, but her sister snorted.

"Not for me. Mama insisted that I learn the pianoforte, but I'm terrible at it. Goldie has all the musical talents in our family, I am afraid."

Was that a jest? Jasper thought it might be and smiled weakly just in case.

He turned to face Marigold again.

"Marigold, your sister tells me that your mother intends to make you marry a man you do not like. Is this true?"

Marigold glanced nervously at her sister, who nodded encouragingly.

"It is true," the young woman murmured, glancing downwards, almost shame-faced.

He nodded. "Well, that is unkind. You ought to be able to choose for yourself. Margaret also tells me that you would rather stay here, with us, rather than go back to live with your mother. Is that true?"

The silence this time was longer, and Marigold seemed even more uncomfortable than before, shifting from foot to foot.

"I must hear it from you, Marigold," he prompted gently, after a moment or two.

Marigold closed her eyes. "I don't want to go home," she said at last. "I love my mother, but I do not... I do not exactly *trust* her at the moment. Or myself. My sister jests about me getting all the musical talent of the family, but *she* has all of the courage. I have none. I would like to stay here, with my sister, if I can."

"I only want my sister to be safe," Margaret murmured. He could feel her eyes burning in his face, sending an uneasy and uncomfortable prickle down his spine. Not unpleasant, exactly, but strange.

"Of course," he acknowledged. Suddenly, he felt like an intruder, one person too many in a room designed for two. "Well, Marigold, you are of course welcome to stay here for as long as you wish, and your sister and I shall do our best to make sure of that. I can promise you this."

Marigold's face brightened with something like hope, and she turned to her sister as if for confirmation.

Jasper cleared his throat, feeling more like a stranger than ever.

"I shall take my leave and allow you two to converse in private."

***

It was one of *those* nights.

Jasper lay awake, staring up at the ceiling in his room. Dinner had been a less uncomfortable affair than usual, with Marigold in good spirits. John had joined them, teasing the younger girl like a sister and telling Margaret about the way various things were done on the farms.

It was almost friendly.

But then the anxiety had come crowding back in, when Marigold started talking about a novel she was reading, which her sister was also reading. John, bless him, did his best to steer the conversation away from literature, but the girls were determined. Jasper was left fidgeting in his seat, praying that *his* opinion wouldn't be asked.

It wasn't, and he wasn't entirely sure whether to be relieved or offended.

And then of course there was the business of the girl. Of Marigold. There *was* a possibility that Lady Keswick might arrive at the house with a magistrate in tow, waving a warrant and demanding that Marigold be turned over to her. And there was a very real possibility that Jasper would not be able to do anything about it.

In a flash, he found himself imagining Margaret's disappointed face. It was his father all over again, with that tight, angry look of disapproval. The final sign that he had let him down once again.

That he had let *her* down.

Groaning aloud, Jasper picked up a pillow and pressed it over his face, trying to block out the moonlight filtering in through the open curtains, and his own thoughts swirling around his head.

If I am going to get between a daughter and a mother, I had better have a very good reason. Well, I believe I do.

In that case, I need to know where I stand legally.

Sighing, Jasper sat up. It was no good – he wasn't going to sleep well tonight. Not until he'd cleared his mind a little.

Pulling on a loose shirt and a pair of trousers, he picked up a candlestick and left his room.

The house was dark and quiet, of course. It was well past midnight, and all the servants were asleep. He tiptoed through the house, holding his breath in case he woke somebody up.

He knew where he needed to go, and what was required. The only way he could familiarize himself with the laws was to read them.

Ugh.

The library was deserted, of course, the cold hanging in the air. The room had been used more frequently since Margaret and her sister arrived, but it was still unfamiliar to Jasper.

Setting his candlestick down on a table, he circled the shelves, lips moving as he slowly sounded out the titles on the index cards. He knew that his father had a great deal of books on family law and so on, if he could just find them.

At last, he found the section he was looking for. The words were engraved on brass plaques, small and neat and difficult to read. There were no less than six books on family law, all heavy, unpleasant-looking tomes. Smothering a sigh, Jasper took out each book and carried it over to a nearby table.

As soon as he opened the first tome, his heart sank. The writing was tiny, the language old-fashioned, the pages crammed with words. It blurred to nothing in front of his eyes. The occasional word showed itself every now and then, only to disappear back into the chaos. It was as if the words were tangling themselves up on the page, and he had to unravel them before he could read a single letter.

It took Jasper about five minutes to decipher the first sentence, and another few minutes to turn it over in his mind, eventually getting the meaning of the words bouncing around in his head.

He pulled up a seat, leaned over the book, and got to work.

This was going to take all night.

Hours had passed. Jasper was so lost in his work, so deep in concentration, that he wasn't aware of footsteps approaching.

"What are you reading?"

He nearly jumped out of his skin, leaping up from the seat and sending the chair skidding backwards.

The woman standing beside him flinched, the candle guttering in her hand.

It was Margaret, of course, her nightgown brushing the floor, a robe wrapped around herself. Her hair was down, falling in thick waves around her shoulders. Her pale face seemed to glow in the gloom. She blinked, clearly taken aback by his reaction.

"I'm sorry, I didn't mean to startle you, I thought you had heard me coming."

He bit his lip, aware that his face was flushing red. "No," he responded, more sharply than he intended.

"I suppose you can't sleep, either," she remarked, leaning over the book he had just been reading. "It's almost dawn, though, so I imagine it's too late to sleep at all. Oh. This is a book on family law?"

He cleared his throat. "Yes. I thought I would do some research on Marigold's situation. John would generally help me, but he's always so busy."

Margaret's face lit up with something like admiration, and she shot a quick, grateful look at him. It made his chest constrict.

"Have you found out anything, yet?"

Had he? All of the information Jasper had carefully deciphered and shelved in his mind disappeared in a flash, and he found himself with nothing to say.

"I... I don't believe so. I've only just started."

She nodded, eyes on the book. He watched enviously as she skimmed down the pages, the words obviously making sense to her at first glance. She flicked through the pages, progressing much farther and much faster than Jasper had managed, until she paused on one particular page.

After a moment, Jasper was able to read the large, printed letters set at the head of the page: *Minor Children And Widowed Mothers.*

It seemed an odd title for a section in a book, but it wasn't as if Jasper was used to this sort of reading.

"What do you think of this part here?" She tapped a particularly lengthy paragraph. "I'm not sure whether it applies to us or not. What do you think? Here, read it."

Jasper could feel sweat beading on his forehead, despite the cold of the room. Swallowing thickly, he leaned forward, staring at the paragraph.

It was a chaotic block of words. He blinked, praying for the words to rearrange themselves before his eyes.

"I..." he swallowed again, trying to work some moisture into his dry throat and mouth. The first line he could make out, it was something about widows and their rights, but then there was a long word which simply would not make sense in his head. He knew, he *knew* that it would be the sort of word he would use in everyday life, something he *understood,* but the marks on the paper simply would not convert themselves to words, to anything coherent.

He risked a glance up, and found Margaret eyeing him, frowning. He dreaded to think what he looked like. Pale, sweaty, visibly terrified, eyes red-rimmed from too much reading and a lack of sleep.

"I'm not sure..." he began again, still praying for the words to make sense.

"Jasper," Margaret said, her voice strange. "Can you not read well? It's a fairly simple paragraph."

Humiliation and anger welled up inside him. Snarling, Jasper slammed the book closed with a *thump* which echoed in the room, very nearly catching Margaret's fingers between the pages. She gave a yelp, leaping back.

"How dare you?" he hissed. "How *dare* you? Of course I can read and write, what gentleman cannot? What sort of duke would I be if I could not *read*? I believe I was very clear to you. I wanted to do my research in private. This is *my* library, and it is *your* sister I am trying to help. I don't require much, duchess, but I did require that you leave me alone to do my research. Are you incapable of following even the simplest instructions?"

She recoiled, blinking in surprise. "Do not speak to me in that manner."

"I shall speak to you in whichever manner I choose. This is my home, and you are my wife. Now get out. Get *out*!"

He pointed towards the door, hand shaking.

Margaret's face had gone white, her lips pressed into a thin, angry line.

"You have made yourself quite clear," she said, voice taut and furious. "Do not worry, *husband*. I'll go. I'll go at once."

And then she stormed out, leaving Jasper standing alone in the silent library, the candle flame guttering. He lowered himself into the seat again, rested his elbows on the table, and dropped his head into his hands.

Chapter Twelve

Margaret was seething. She stamped up to her room, not caring how loud she was. Quickly, she changed out of her night things into a simple walking dress, pulling on her boots herself and nearly falling over in the process.

Part of her wanted to take out a bag and start stuffing her clothes into it. Why would she stay somewhere with a man who spoke to her that way and had such an explosive temper? His words still rang in her head.

"I shall speak to you in whichever manner I choose. This is my home, and you are my wife. Now get out. Get out!"

"I'll get out, all right," she muttered.

She did not, of course, take out a bag and begin packing. What would be the point? She had nowhere to go, except back to her mother's house, and *that* was out of the question.

Outside, the sky was just beginning to lighten. Dawn was still a little way off, the sun not touching the horizon yet, but Margaret did not care. She needed to get out. She needed to walk. Needed to *move*.

That was how she had managed to keep a cool head during all the arguments she had had with her mother over the years. She went outside and she walked until the anger had mostly drained away. There was no reason why things should be any different here.

***

There was no night footman on duty, so Margaret unlocked the heavy front door herself and slipped out into the early morning light.

There were probably quieter, smaller side doors she could have let herself out of, but Margaret still hadn't gotten used to the maze of Stonehaven above stairs, let alone the busy maze of the servants' stairs and corridors.

She walked quickly, head down, breath frosting in the air in front of her. Frost glimmered on the fields, and the world was all in black and white. The sky held a pale greyish tint, promising the oncoming sunrise. Margaret's steps crunched on the frost, and her hem dragged along the ground.

The cold, refreshing air and the peaceful silence worked their magic. As always, when she'd gone for walks to calm herself down, Margaret felt the tension seeping out of her limbs. Her shoulders lowered, she breathed more deeply and slowly, and some of her anger faded.

He shouldn't have spoken to her like that, of course not. But perhaps she had been too blunt. Had he really been sitting in that library all night, reading? Studying, to prepare for taking on the guardianship of *her* sister?

Margaret's steps faltered, and she found herself remembering the way Jasper had looked when she first saw him. He had been leaning over that heavy, dense old book, brow furrowed, dark circles under his eyes, lips moving.

And then there'd been the humiliation and frustration in his face when he tried to read that paragraph she pointed out. It had been so clear that he did not understand it, that he *could* not understand.

Can he truly not read? He must be able to read a little.

But he was so angry.

Margaret closed her eyes. No, not angry. At least, not just angry. He was humiliated. Embarrassed. Frustrated.

He can't read. Or at least, not well.

Why on earth not? Wouldn't a duke have access to the finest tutors as a child? Wouldn't he have had all the opportunities to learn?

She sighed, pressing the heels of her hands against her eyes. Margaret was exhausted, the tiredness suddenly piling on her. Whatever mistakes she had made, he had still shouted at *her* and ordered her out.

Part of her wanted to go back to her room and sleep for a few more hours, but the restlessness had set in, and she already knew that she wouldn't sleep.

Besides, it would be nice to see the sunrise.

Taking a sharp left, Margaret headed into a narrow path which led through a little wooded area. She knew that it would lead up the hill and towards a pretty little gazebo, from which she would get an excellent view of the sun rising. Besides, it was light enough to see where she was going.

That, it turned out, was not quite true. The forest was darker than she had expected, and sound seemed to be muffled.

For the first time, Margaret felt a prickle of uneasiness along her spine. She cleared her throat, holding her head high, and tried to step a little faster.

Was it her imagination, or were there echoing footsteps following her through the woods?

Don't be a fool, she scolded herself. *It's most likely an echo.*

Sure enough, whenever her feet crunched down through the layer of frost on the earth, an answering footstep echoed behind her. She paused, listening, but there was only silence.

However, when she started walking again, the echoes begun. That should have reassured her that they *were* echoes, but instead of feeling better, Margaret felt... well, she felt as though she were being followed.

She bit the inside of her cheek, trying to keep a steady pace. Looking behind her was a bad idea, of course. Once a person had looked behind them once, they were obliged to keep doing so. It never helped to dispel the idea of being followed, or watched, or otherwise in danger.

Are you afraid of wolves or bears?

That was a silly thought. Margaret had conjured it up to try and mock herself out of her fear, but it only highlighted what *truly* frightened her.

And that, of course, was people. Men, specifically. Bandits and highwaymen weren't in the business of often barging on ducal lands at dawn, but there was a first time for everything, wasn't there?

She paused again to listen, and this time, she could have sworn that a few of the footsteps fell *after* she had stopped. Not echoes, then.

You're a fool. Just frightening yourself.

Sharp self-scoldings were not working, it seemed. The fears persisted.

Knowing full well that it was a bad idea, Margaret spun around to look behind her.

Nothing. The silvery path wound along, quiet and deserted. She waited, listening while her heart was pounding.

And then, slowly and quite clearly, a twig cracked somewhere behind her.

Margaret couldn't help it. She broke into a run, hoicking her skirts up almost to her knees, and raced along the frosty path. Her feet skidded on the frost, and she nearly lost her balance more than once. The footsteps only increased in pace – which they would do, if they were echoes, but also if she were being chased – and Margaret bit back a cry of fear.

At last, at *last*, she burst out of the woodland, nearly tripping on the stony path. She twisted around to look behind her as she ran.

Was it her imagination, or was there a shadowy shape in the trees behind her? No, no, surely not. That would make it all real, and at the moment Margaret was still frantically trying to convince herself that it was only her wild imagination that had conjured up the threat.

After a few moments of breathless running up the sparse hillside, it was clear that she was *not* being followed. An assailant might stay hidden in the woodland, but there was no cover between the treeline and the gazebo. Still, Margaret kept running, now wheezing for breath, climbing up and up.

She staggered into the circular gazebo, footsteps ringing out hollowly on the stone floor. She twisted around, half-expecting to see a mysterious, armed figure appear from nowhere, face swathed in a scarf and a blade glinting in his hand.

You have been reading too many novels, my girl. You would scold Goldie for this sort of thing.

Margaret leaned back against one of the pillars, trying desperately to catch her breath. Her lungs felt as though they were on fire. She closed her eyes, trying to calm her pounding heart.

"Your Grace?"

Margaret gave an undignified squeak, leaping what felt like several yards into the air.

She spun around to face the man who had appeared just off to her right, and immediately relaxed.

John Locke stood there, dressed for the cold, his breath misting in front of him. He had a cap onto his head, and hastily snatched it off.

"John," she gasped. "Mr. Locke. It's you. I thought... well, I rather thought I was being followed. But I suppose it was just you."

John smiled wryly. "I am sorry if I startled you. Actually, his Grace sent me out to find you. He said that you had gone out for a walk, and he was concerned about your safety. It is still dark, and one can slip and get hurt quite badly, even close to the house."

Margaret flushed. "I'm not entirely useless, you know."

John bit his lip. "I didn't say that you were, Your Grace."

She immediately felt guilty. "I apologise, I ought not to have been so sharp in my tone. I merely... experienced a rather unsettling fright, you see?"

He nodded. "Of course, of course. Would you like me to take a look around?"

"No, no, of course not. Tell me, which way did you come up to the gazebo?"

"Just over the ridge. I saw you run out of the woodland and up here."

The hairs prickled on the back of Margaret's neck. So John was *not* the one who'd followed her through the woodland.

Nobody followed you through the woodland, she scolded herself angrily. *Don't be foolish.*

She cleared her throat, running her hand over her hair. She hadn't bothered to put it up properly for her walk and had only twined it back into a braid.

"So, Jasper told you to come after me," she said, carefully. "What exactly did he say?"

John wavered, looking as though he couldn't decide how to explain. At last, he sighed, raking a hand through his hair.

"I should tell you, Your Grace, that the duke confides in me about most things."

"He told you, then."

John shrugged. "Indeed. He told me."

"He told you that I was sharp with him, and ungrateful over the help he was giving to my sister, and accused him of being… of being *illiterate*? And then he shouted at me and ordered me out, and now here I am. He told you that?"

John grimaced. "More or less, indeed. He did not characterize you as sharp or ungrateful, I assure you. I believe you are excessively critical of yourself, much as he is of his own merits."

Margaret sighed, suddenly feeling entirely drained of energy. She wished she hadn't raced up the hillside like a fool. Already she was dreading the slow, slippery trip back *down* the hillside. She prayed she wouldn't fall and slide right down the bottom. That would be *too* humiliating.

"We are not compatible, I think," she said tiredly. "I don't know what to do next."

John took a moment to respond, chewing his lower lip.

"I think you have more in common than you believe, Your Grace, I think that there is something you should know. You said that the duke seemed unable to read or write, yes?"

"I didn't mean…"

"He can read, just about, and write. However, it is extremely difficult for him. As a boy, it took him far longer to learn to read than other boys his age. The words simply do not make sense in his head. Writing is a chore, and reading seems to be like translating from a different language for him."

Margaret blinked. "What? But he seems so intelligent."

"He is. That's the confusing thing. I have known the duke for years, Your Grace. He *is* a clever man, and a remarkably quick study. He excels at most subjects and did so at school. That made his inability to learn to read and write all the more baffling. Most of his tutors gave up on him. His father…" John trailed off, his expression hardening. "Well. The old duke decided that his son was simple-minded. Nothing could have been further from the truth, but he believed it, and treated him accordingly. I'm sure you can imagine how his Grace was treated."

Margaret certainly could. Even in her own finishing school, she'd seen how certain girls with less ability in certain areas had been treated. She had never been able to grasp the intricacies of music, for instance. Women like Lady Alice and Goldie could coax the most delightful tunes out of a pianoforte and could learn complex pieces with ease.

The few tunes Margaret had been able to learn were simple and almost childish, thumped out on the keys with little grace and no timing at all. She simply was not cut out for music, much as she might appreciate hearing good music played.

She could only imagine how a duke's only son would be treated, if he proved incapable of learning to read.

"It's strange," she murmured. "A man so intelligent being unable to *read*, of all things."

John shrugged. "It is not unheard of. It is as if there's some sort of mental block, something *stopping* his natural development in that respect. I can't make sense of it. If his Grace were simple-minded, it would make sense, but he is most decidedly not. Perhaps if he had had different tutors in his youth, perhaps ones that relied less on threats and violence and more on unconventional teachings, his development might have been different. It's too late, of course. Even now, his Grace struggles to read and write. I help him as much as I can, but of course I cannot always be there."

Margaret bit her lip, remembering the pile of old law-books stacked up beside Jasper. She remembered the concentration on his face, the horror and humiliation when she had asked him if he could not read.

"I have handled it badly, I think," she said, after a pause. "I believe I hurt his feelings."

"You weren't to know. His Grace hides it well. Understandably, he does not want people to know about this."

"Of course. I shan't tell anyone," Margaret assured John at once, and the man relaxed a little.

"I'm glad. Indeed, I didn't imagine that you would betray his confidence."

There was a brief silence between them. The sun was just below the horizon now, casting a delicate blush of pink and gold upon the sky, heralding a most splendid dawn. Margaret leaned back against a pillar, resting her head against the cold stone.

"I wish to speak with him," she heard herself declare. "I desire to lay all of this bare.

We are married, for heaven's sake. We cannot continue to behave as strangers in

our own home. A change is necessary, particularly if we are to pursue guardianship

of my sister. It is remarkably generous of him to acquiesce to such an arrangement,

I must say."

John gave a wry smile. "His Grace is the best of men, you know. It might be hard to see it at the moment, but I believe you and he will suit each other perfectly."

Margaret snorted. "We shall see."

Chapter Thirteen

A man stood in the shadows of the treeline, watching the new Duchess of Stonehaven race up the hillside, away from him.

He didn't follow her. She'd see him at once, and he had no orders beyond watching her and reporting back.

Besides, there was another man nearby, a lanky fellow walking along the ridge of the hillside. He would have seen the Duchess too, and they would likely meet up at an ugly little stone building on the tip of the hill.

He stayed motionless, watching the scene unfold. the Duchess reached the stone building, gasping for breath and obviously nervous.

Perhaps I was clumsier than usual. Well, it's hardly my fault. I'm a valet, not a hired assassin.

Hoggins wished he had not conjured up the idea of assassinations and such. His master hadn't seen fit to confide his plans to his valet, and Hoggins had only been instructed to spend the night watching Stonehaven Manor, to watch the movements of the inhabitants carefully, and report everything back. It wasn't the first time he had been given this assignment, and it was unlikely to be the last.

The Duchess' sudden, pre-dawn walk had been something of a surprise. He had seen lights on in the window which looked into the library, but hadn't dared get close enough to peer in. And then, just as he was thinking of abandoning his watch and going home, the Duchess came striding out of the house, clearly furious and heading nowhere in particular.

It had been obvious that he should follow her. The wretched frost made everything crisp, his footsteps far louder than they should have been, but it was too late to go back and change things.

Extremely carefully, Hoggins withdrew from the tree line, and hurried back through the woodland. With the sun coming up, he was not about to risk getting caught. His master would not come to save him if he were discovered. In fact, he would deny all knowledge of anything he had commanded Hoggins to do.

At a respectable distance from Stonehaven Manor, Hoggins summoned a hired coach. Hiring coaches was a luxury he did not usually allow himself, but his master had given him money for it. Apparently, he was eager to hear whatever information he had to share.

Not that there was much worth sharing, in point of fact. Hoggins climbed into the coach, grimacing. He wondered if he would be in trouble for not bringing any useful information back.

It's hardly my fault. They're a dull family. They don't go anywhere. The girl is never left alone, not for a moment, not unless we want to break into the house.

That's probably too risky. Probably.

"Where to?" the coach driver asked shortly, voice hoarse with lack of sleep and too much gin. The streets were busy already – life began early for the poorer folk of London. Few people could afford to lie in till noon, like the gentry did.

"Keswick House," Hoggins responded shortly. "And get me there fast. There's no time to lose."

***

A carriage pulled up outside the house. Lady Keswick let the curtain fall back into place, heart thumping.

It had been a long night.

"Not going to finish the game, then? We've another hand left, by my calculations," Lord Tumnus spoke up. He'd filled the room with cigar smoke and the scent of alcohol, streaming off his clothing and from his breath. Lady Keswick relished a modest glass of brandy on occasion, and appreciated a fine vintage as much as any discerning palate, yet, truly, the gentleman indulged in excess.

"Your man is back," she responded, voice cool and clipped, careful not to betray any emotion. "I imagine he has nothing new to tell us. I'm not sure it was necessary to stay up all night waiting for his return."

Lord Tumnus chuckled, dropping the cards onto the baize card-table, mixing with the ash of his cigar.

"It's easier to stay up late than get up early, in my experience."

"Your experience is not universal, Lord Tumnus."

"No," he said, clamping the cigar between his teeth, "But it is established that I am making the decisions here, is it not? And I do so enjoy your company, my dear Lady Keswick."

She fought not to roll her eyes. At times, it seemed like the man enjoyed taunting her. No, he almost certainly did.

How could I ever have believed he was a suitable match for sweet Marigold?

It was too late to think of such things. It was *far beyond* too late.

Out in the hallway, Lady Keswick could hear muffled voices. The valet talking with the night footman, no doubt. With the Duke of Stonehaven's generous allowance – more generous than she could have imagined – she was able to pay off most of the servants and even consider hiring some new ones. She had treated herself to some fine bottles of wine, only to have wretched Lord Tumnus gulp them down in the first hour of his visit. No doubt he barely tasted them. He had said once that the cigars and brandy tended to dull his sense of taste.

And yet he drank my good wine, even so. Wretch.

She retreated to her seat by the fire, which was almost out, and managed to settle down and compose herself before the valet appeared. The valet knocked, and Lord Tumnus allowed him to enter. As if it were his decision to make! As if he owned the house already!

Lady Keswick bit into her lower lip until she tasted copper, curling her fingers into fists to control herself.

Indeed, my dear Margaret, you often wondered where you got your temper from. Well, you got it from me, of course. Only, I have learned to control mine. I was forced to, after all.

The valet came mincing in, bringing in a wave of cold air with him. He smelled of manure and sweat, and Lady Keswick wrinkled her nose.

"Well, man? Any news?" Lord Tumnus demanded briskly.

"Can't I have a cup of tea, first?" the valet bleated, arms wrapped tight around himself. "It was freezing out there."

"After. Go on, let's hear it."

Lady Keswick closed her eyes. It helped her listen, sometimes.

The valet – she never could remember his name – never had much new information to share. But then, this business of spying on Stonehaven was a fairly new one. Marigold did not leave the house, or at least had not left the house yet. She occasionally took walks in the garden, but not after dark, and never alone.

The duke was nearly always at home, except when he visited tenant farmers and so on. However, those visits were irregular and difficult to predict. Since Margaret was still in her honeymoon period, she was of course not paying or receiving visits yet, and she rarely left the house, either.

Lady Keswick could have told them this already. Stonehaven was a vast place, with endless rooms and entertainments. She'd heard that the previous Duchess of Stonehaven – the current duke's mother, long deceased, of course – had been a great proficient in the field of music, with a fantastic music room which was much talked about. Lady Keswick remembered the talk, and the gossip when the Duchess' health refused to allow her to practise her music. Once Marigold stumbled upon that room, there would be no tearing her away.

A flash of anger and jealousy tore through Lady Keswick.

We had to sell our pianoforte. Not that we got much for it. And Marigold cried for days.

Well, once the wretched girl married Lord Tumnus, she could have pianofortes in every room, if she chose. He would give her whatever she wanted, after all. To start with, at least. If Marigold was clever, she would get what she could out of the old man, before his interest started to wane.

Not that Marigold has ever been clever. Pretty, yes, sweet, indeed, but clever? No.

"So, nothing new," Lord Tumnus interrupted. The valet faltered, cut off in mid-flow.

"Well, no, your lordship. Not much. Except that the Duchess went for a walk before dawn this morning."

"That does not help us," Lord Tumnus snarled, getting to his feet. "It's not the Duchess we are interested in. It's the girl. Miss Marigold, the pretty, young one. What did you see of her tonight?"

The hapless valet shuffled his feet, looking miserable. "Not much, your lordship. Nothing at all, I'd say."

Lord Tumnus growled. "Useless. Go on down to the kitchen and wake up some of the maids. They'll make you breakfast, I daresay. Not that you deserve it. I shall inform you when I have another task for you."

The poor valet bowed and shuffled out of the room without another word. Lady Keswick felt a stab of sympathy for him.

That, of course, was dangerous. She had better keep all of her sympathy for herself. She was going to need it.

"Waste of time," Lord Tumnus muttered. "Still, he'll chance upon something useful, if we are just a little patient. The girl will be left unattended sooner or later, I'm sure."

Lady Keswick bit back a sigh. "I fear that you are going to be disappointed, Lord Tumnus. You underestimate the stubbornness of my daughter. My *older* daughter, that is. Margaret is tenacious and remarkably clever. She is determined to keep Marigold from you."

"However, securing the girl was *your* responsibility, was it not?" the man shot back, lips curling. "You cannot control either of your daughters, it seems. But no matter. You are Marigold's mother and guardian. If you give your consent for the marriage, that is all that matters, legally. We just need to get our hands on her."

Not for the first time, guilt tightened Lady Keswick's chest. She pushed it aside as best she could.

"Marigold may not wish to come," she said carefully. "If she refuses to come with us…"

"We shan't give her the choice. It is easier that way. Why waste time arguing with servants, children, and one's inferiors, eh?"

He chuckled, pouring himself another generous measure of brandy.

Lady Keswick got to her feet, crossing to the window again. She felt vaguely sick.

It was quite dark outside still and light inside, meaning that she could only see her own reflection. She had only seen the carriage because of the lantern swinging on its side.

She heard the creak of floorboards behind her, and knew that Lord Tumnus had crossed the room silently, and now stood directly behind her. Sure enough, his round, florid face appeared in the window, reflected.

"I am not sure I like your attitude, Lady K.," he said, voice deceptively soft. "If you recall, you and I had a deal. You have not held up your part, but I have been remarkably patient. Don't you think? Everything was simple – I would marry the girl, and in return, you would get your freedom. The debts in my study with your name upon them will be struck off, destroyed, as if they never existed. Won't that be a fine thing? Imagine it. Fix that day in your mind, and perhaps that will energise you into keeping your promise. Because you promised that I would marry Marigold, Lady Keswick."

She saw the familiar greed light up his eyes when he spoke of Marigold. It was getting harder and harder to convince herself it was a simple feeling of love, and not something darker and crueler. Marigold was a sweet girl, but women *needed* rich husbands. Better that she married an old rake like Lord Tumnus, who at least was rich and powerful, than some poor youth without prospects.

Saying nothing in response, Lady Keswick made to turn away, but Lord Tumnus wrapped a meaty hand around her shoulder, turning her to face him.

"I spoke to you, my dear," he said, voice sharp. His breath stunk of cigars, and Lady Keswick fought not to wrinkle her nose. "It is only polite to answer."

Lady Keswick swallowed hard. "I cannot simply walk into that house and take my daughter back. They have the protection of the Duke of Stonehaven, who is not a man to be trifled with."

Lord Tumnus scowled, and she was able to yank her shoulder free.

It was fairly clear that the dear man did not particularly like the duke. No, more to the point, he was *afraid* of him. And rightly so, perhaps. Lady Keswick did not know the Duke of Stonehaven well, but he had a fearsome reputation.

If he had only married Marigold, she thought, with a stab of anger, *then none of this would have happened. But no, he wanted Margaret. Heaven only knows why.*

Lady Keswick resolutely forced down any thoughts of her oldest daughter. She had replayed their conversations in her head over and over again. She saw Margaret's baffled, angry expression, unable to understand why her mother refused to give in over this matter. Of course, it was obvious that Marigold was too good for a man like Lord Tumnus, money notwithstanding.

It was no longer about that, however.

"Well, we need a plan, then," Lord Tumnus said, following Lady Keswick back to the card table. She set about collecting up the cards, gently brushing each one free of cigar ash. They were a rather fine set, a present from her husband. He'd always known how much she enjoyed playing cards.

I enjoyed it rather too much, I think. It seems that cards have been my downfall.

Some of the cards were sticky, no doubt from drops of brandy, but there was not much to be done about that. She would wipe them down later, after the wretched man had left. *If* he ever left.

"So long as the duke is supporting Margaret and Marigold, we are virtually powerless," she heard herself say. "We must separate Margaret and the duke. Without his support, there is very little she can do if I choose to bring Marigold home."

"And what if he doesn't stop giving his aid?" Lord Tumnus demanded sourly. "They are newly married, after all. Their honeymoon is not even finished. I daresay he'll be doting on her for months yet."

Lady Keswick allowed herself a small smile. "On the contrary, my Lord. My daughter is quite headstrong, and the good Duke is equally so. It is but a question of time before they grow weary of one another—or, ideally, come to an impasse. We must bide our time."

"I am not a patient man. And those debts of yours are gathering interest continuously. If I choose to call them in..."

He trailed off, not finishing the thought. Not that he needed to. Lady Keswick's blood ran cold, but she held her composure.

"I shall try periodically to bring Marigold home," Lady Keswick assured him, carefully keeping her eyes on the cards. How much would a set like this be worth? A good amount, she imagined. "All will be well, Lord Tumnus. Just wait a little longer."

"As long as it is not more than a little longer," he groused. "I ought to have married the girl weeks ago."

Lady Keswick tasted bile. She finished tidying up the card table and moved back to the window. Like before, only her own reflection greeted her.

The Duke of Stonehaven would never help her, not now. Nobody would help her. She would have to keep her promise, and she had promised Marigold to Lord Tumnus.

What have I done? Oh, God, what have I done?

Chapter Fourteen

Jasper's own words rolled round and round in his head, taunting him. He had spent quite some time mulling them over, as the sun gradually rose outside, light filtering through the grimy panes of the library windows.

"How dare you? How dare you? Of course I can read and write, what gentleman cannot? What sort of duke would I be if I could not read? I believe I was very clear to you. I wanted to do my research in private. This is my library, and it is your sister I am trying to help. I don't require much, duchess, but I did require that you leave me alone to do my research. Are you incapable of following even the simplest instructions?"

He could still see the shocked, hurt expression on Margaret's face, the furrow appearing between her brows.

"Do not speak to me in that manner."

"I shall speak to you in whichever manner I choose." His response had been swift, spoken almost without thinking. He still remembered how he'd taken a step forward, finger stabbing the air in Margaret's direction. *"This is my home, and you are my wife. Now get out. Get out!"*

Jasper closed his eyes, dropping his head into his hands.

He was still in the library, although he had long since given up on researching. The words in the heavy legal tomes were starting to hurt his eyes, and he couldn't make sense of them in any case. He wasn't much further forward, but he had established that there were precedents in both cases – widows wresting control of children from male guardians and relatives, and male guardians separating widows from children in turn. Divorced women, of course, had no rights to anything, not even their own children.

Lady Keswick was not divorced. She could indeed give her consent on Marigold's behalf for the girl to be married, and it would hold legal weight. And, at the end of it, if the marriage had gone forward and been consummated – he shuddered on Marigold's behalf – the judge would likely instruct that Marigold stay with her new husband, and some damages would be paid. That would not help Marigold. Not one bit.

He was still puzzling over the situation when a gentle knock at the door jerked him out of his reverie.

"Come in."

The door inched open, revealing Mrs. Nettle carrying a tea tray.

"I had a little trouble finding you, Your Grace," she said mildly. "You are usually in your study at this hour."

"I'm sorry, I should have sent word," he mumbled, rubbing his eyes. "Is the Duchess...?"

"She returned to her room a little while ago, Your Grace. John escorted her. Do you know if her Grace intends to make a habit of early morning walks? I might suggest she take a maid with her. The grounds can be treacherous in the dark."

Jasper grimaced. "I doubt she'll make a habit of it. But then, what do I know?"

Mrs. Nettle eyed him for a moment, and Jasper guessed that his tone of voice gave away his feelings. She sighed and set the tea tray down on the table in front of him.

"Do you know anything about apologising, Janey?" Jasper asked, face still buried in his hands.

She sighed again. "I know that honesty is crucial, as is frankness. If you intend to apologise, don't make excuses. Don't over-explain your behaviour. Indeed, certain factors may have contributed to something you have said or done, but at the end of the day, you bear the responsibility for your own actions. Shoulder that responsibility like an adult. Don't let too much time go by before the apology is made. Don't be half-hearted. Don't be defensive."

He glanced up at her. "That is a lot of advice."

She shrugged. "Most of it is common sense. If I may be so bold, Your Grace, is there a problem with the Duchess?"

"Yes. I was... rude to her. Very blunt and a little harsh. She made a comment about my reading. Nothing unkind, but I reacted badly. Then she stormed off on that early-morning walk. If she had anywhere else to go, I shouldn't be surprised if she packed her things and left altogether."

He glanced up properly, meeting Mrs. Nettle's eye. He was a little afraid he would read judgement there, or disapproval, but Janey was just as cool and composed as always. He thought he saw sympathy in her face.

"Oh, dear," she sighed. "Well, I'm sorry for it, Your Grace. You are a strong character, and so is the Duchess. While it's not for me to say, of course, I'm sure that if you are frank and honest with her, she will forgive you. She doesn't strike me as the sort of person to hold a grudge. Besides, they need your help if they are to keep Miss Marigold safe."

Jasper flinched. He hadn't thought of that. Was it possible that Margaret felt that he was holding his influence over her head? He wasn't, of course, but surely she couldn't be happy with her reliance on him. Jasper was well aware that if he withdrew his influence, Marigold might be taken back into her mother's custody.

"I should reassure her that I still intend to help Marigold," he said slowly, and Mrs. Nettle nodded.

"I think her Grace would appreciate that. And so would Miss Marigold."

"You're right. I'll... I'll speak to her today. Is she still asleep?"

"I believe so, Your Grace, but she has taken to writing letters after breakfast in the orange morning-room, while Miss Marigold practices her music. You might find the chance to speak to her then."

Jasper smiled in relief. "I shall talk to her. And thank you, Janey."

Mrs Nettle smiled, dimples showing, and for a moment, Jasper once again saw the plain, serious young woman who'd done so much to help him learn to read and write.

"The pleasure is mine, Your Grace."

***

The orange morning room was not a favourite room of Jasper's. It was just a little too... well, too *orange*. Still, Margaret seemed to have taken to it. He could hear her quill scratching away as he stood before the door. He drew in a breath, briefly rehearsing the apology he'd lined up in his head, and knocked.

The writing sound stopped.

"Who is it?"

"It's me, Margaret."

He heard an impatient sigh. It was hardly an invitation to come in, but he pushed open the door anyway. Margaret was still bent over her writing desk, despite the fact that she clearly was not writing anything.

"Go away," she said shortly. "I am not speaking to you."

"Don't be childish, Margaret."

She whipped around to face him, glaring balefully. "*Childish*? You nearly severed my head over a mere remark. I did not intend to offend you. Nevertheless, I am grateful for the stern reminder that all within this abode, myself included, is entirely yours."

He flushed. "I should not have said that. I should not have snapped. I... I'm sorry, Margaret. That's what I came here for. I'm here to apologise."

She blinked at him, clearly taken aback. "Truly? You are really here to apologise?"

He held out his arms at his sides. "I shouldn't have spoken sharply. I'm not surprised you were angry."

She seemed to deflate a little. "Well, I suppose it's just my pride that was hurt. You *are* doing a great deal to help Goldie, after all."

"You accept my apology, then?"

She smiled tentatively. "Of course. I didn't mean to insult you, really."

"You didn't."

There. He'd said it. The apology was done. There was a pause, and Jasper found himself shifting from foot to foot uncertainly. Should he leave? Margaret hadn't resumed writing and was looking up at him expectantly.

Leave, he thought. *Just let the apology sit with her. She doesn't want your company.*

You have work to do, back in your study.

He thought of the piles of papers awaiting his attention, and grimaced. Margaret was still looking at him. Waiting.

He sighed, closing his eyes.

"The truth is, I *do* struggle with reading and writing. I always have."

Margaret blinked, seeming surprised. "But you seem so intelligent." She immediately flushed. "I didn't mean to imply that you weren't... oh, I'm sorry. Sit down, please."

She indicated an empty seat nearby, and he took it, not entirely sure where the conversation was supposed to be going.

"I'm not offended," he sighed. "When it comes to mathematics, or history, or science, or any other subjects, I'm more than quick enough. I can remember things very well. But for as long as I can remember, reading has been incredibly difficult for me. Other children my age learned easily, and I just... I just never could."

Margaret considered this. "When you say *difficult*, what do you mean?"

"The words move," he said at last. "They seem to wiggle around on the page. Others have told me that when they read and write, they can *hear* the words sound out in their head. I have never had that. I have to concentrate hard to understand even one sentence. Writing is just as difficult. Even now, my writing is riddled with spelling mistakes. John has to look over and rewrite every single letter and paper I send. I don't understand why I struggle. Nobody did, least of all my father. He made his feelings clear on having a simpleton for a son."

Margaret leaned forward, and for a moment, he thought she was going to take his hand in hers. At the last moment, however, she seemed to change her mind, folding her hands together in her lap instead.

"You aren't a simpleton," she said staunchly. "Anybody who has the pleasure of making your acquaintance shall be well aware of that."

"You say that," he murmured, "but once society learns of my limited abilities in reading and writing, their regard for me diminishes most swiftly, I assure you."

"Not people who *matter*. I haven't known you long, Jasper, but *I* know that you aren't a simpleton. I value your advice, and I know you are an intelligent man. It's strange that you struggle so much with reading and writing, but you cannot be the sole individual in the world who possesses a …. a weakness."

He glanced up at her, smiling wryly. "A weakness?"

"Indeed, something that one would expect to accomplish with ease, as others do with little effort, yet for some reason, it proves most challenging. We are all different, and sometimes our strengths and weaknesses seem to be at the whims of chance. For me, I struggle with music. Goldie took to playing music like a fish to water. She loves playing the pianoforte, and she is *very* good at it. I'm no less intelligent than she is, but I simply do *not* have the talent for music. My mind is not well-suited for it, I fear, despite my earnest efforts. Whenever I endeavour to play the piano, it resembles nothing more than a cat traipsing across the keys."

He had to chuckle at that, and Margaret smiled, clearly glad she'd cheered him up.

"There is a difference between music and reading," he answered wryly. "One can go through life without playing the pianoforte, or without being very good at it, but reading and writing are other things altogether. Especially with an estate like mine to run."

"That is true," she acknowledged, "And that *is* unfortunate. But the plain fact is that we are all different, and all of us are better at some things than others. You aren't a simpleton, and so it is."

"I do love your confidence," he said, smiling. "And thank you, Margaret. I… I'm glad to hear you say that. My father, my tutors at Eton, the tutors he engaged at home, all thought I was simply dull, or else that I wouldn't apply myself. I think I believed them, for quite a while. After some time, they realized that whippings and beatings and various other punishments were having no effect, and eventually gave up."

Margaret bit her lip. "That's terrible. I've never understood why schoolmasters and parents think that their children will do better after being *beaten*."

Jasper shrugged. "It taught me to be strong, I think. Taught me to rely on myself. I'm quite well now, you see."

Margaret shot him a quick, calculating look, and it struck Jasper that he was *not* quite well, and she did not believe it any more than he believed it himself. Clearing his throat, he looked away.

"Perhaps I could teach you," she burst out.

He blinked at her in surprise. "I beg your pardon?"

Margaret coloured. "I mean, of course you can *already* read and write, but you say you find it difficult. I'm generally a good teacher, people say, and I *am* good at reading and writing. Perhaps there's a way of making it simpler for you. If you'd like to try, that is."

Jasper paused, considering. He immediately thought of the humiliations of his youth. Of mocking laughter from his schoolmates, and outrage from his tutors. Of being caned, of having his palms switched, of being beaten, or made to miss meals, or stand on stools in the corner of the room with a *simpleton* sign around his neck. Oh, he could recollect every excruciating detail of every humiliation, every punishment that he *knew*, deep down, that he did not deserve.

Then he glanced at Margaret, who was watching him hopefully, earnestly. He felt a wave of affection so intense he had to look away, so badly did he want to reach over and sweep her into his arms.

She holds me in regard, he thought, with a jarring epiphany. *It is not mere pretence. She genuinely cares for my well-being. She is vexed by the ill treatment I have endured. She does not perceive me as a simpleton.*

Perhaps I'm not one, after all.

"Very well, then," he heard himself say, heart thumping inside his chest as if it were trying to get out. "I can't promise I'll learn any better, but I will try. There... there was one tutor who seemed to be helping. His name was Mr. Pippin, but most of the other teachers thought he was too soft. He never caned the boys, you know, or shouted or threw things. He was a very kind man and took pains with me. I sometimes think I only learned the alphabet at all because of his help."

Margaret smiled at him. "Then we know what is likely to work for you, then. I shall try and follow in the footsteps of Mr. Pippin. You're a grown man now, and you can learn as much or as little as you like."

He let out a long, slow breath. *I certainly didn't think, when I came here to apologise, that I would walk out with a reading lesson planned.*

"Thank you," he said aloud. "You're very kind, Margaret."

She smiled. "You deserve kindness, Jasper. Everybody does. I think we forget that, far too often."

Chapter Fifteen

Three Days Later

"A party," Jasper said at last. "*Here*. The day after tomorrow."

Margaret smiled hopefully. "It's rather late notice, but a small, informal gathering might be suggested, and people would come, I'm sure. Mrs. Nettle thinks that it could be arranged in time."

Jasper's gaze flicked over her shoulder, landing on the demure and silent Mrs. Nettle. His eyebrows raised questioningly, and Mrs. Nettle gave the tiniest nod.

"It could be managed, Your Grace," she said. "I believe Miss Marigold would enjoy it."

Margaret was glad that Mrs. Nettle had agreed to come along with her. It was likely that Jasper would be more inclined to listen to his old friend and trusted housekeeper.

Although, having said that, he and Margaret *had* been getting on a great deal better than before. In the three days since their long, serious conversation, they had conducted two reading lessons together. Things had been stiff, and rather awkward, but Margaret was convinced that with a little time, things would grow easier between them. The lessons had happened in the library, with an expanse of mahogany desk between them. Jasper leaned over his papers with an air of determination and concentration, and Margaret hardly dared speak for fear of disturbing his focus.

He held his quill nicely and gracefully, like a gentleman, but she saw at once how difficult writing was for him. The words emerged laboriously from the nib of his quill, accompanied by numerous crossings-out and misspelling.

He said he had a headache by the end of their first lesson, but there was no talk of giving up. Not yet, at least.

It didn't feel as though they were husband and wife, surely not, but Margaret couldn't help but feel as though they were *friends*, or heading that way.

He is handsome. After some time, why shouldn't we grow a little closer than friends?

She had thought that sort of thing to herself more often than she cared to remember, heart thudding and face flushing with a sort of guilt that did not entirely make sense.

Concentrate, Margaret. Focus.

Jasper sighed, passing a hand over his hair. "A *party*? Here? I can't remember the last time we threw a party here. I certainly didn't enjoy it, whatever it was."

"It's to help Goldie with her come-out," Margaret explained. "She's nervous, and it isn't a good idea to keep her away from Society for too long."

Jasper sighed, leaning back in his seat. They were in Jasper's study, the curtains thrown open to let in the golden swathes of brisk morning light. The air outside was deceptively chilly, a layer of frost still lying over the fields. It would soon melt under the sunshine, however, and it would be as though the frost was never there at all.

"I suppose I'd have to attend, if you did have a party," Jasper muttered.

Margaret bit her lip. "Well, yes. We both would. We'd need to lend Goldie our respectability and our name. Your name," she corrected, and ploughed on. "You could go and play cards in the billiards room with your friends, if you preferred. Mrs. Nettle recommended a few card-tables, and while there will be dancing, *you* won't be expected to dance."

"I should hope not," he shot back, ungracefully. "As to playing cards with my friends, I don't have any. Friends, that is. But if you really think a party is the right thing to do – and if you think people will attend – then you can send out the invitations."

Margaret blinked, not quite able to grasp for a moment that she'd gotten her way.

"Truly? You really mean it?"

Jasper met her eye and smiled wryly. "I'm not in the habit of making promises I can't keep. So long as I'm not troubled with the preparations, you can do as you like. It's your house, too."

Margaret beamed, turning to grin at Mrs. Nettle. She had the chance to see a small, triumphant smile on the housekeeper's face, just for an instant, before it was gone and the usual cool composure was back.

"I shall begin the preparations at once," Mrs. Nettle said blandly. "Will you inform me of how many guests there will be, Your Grace?"

"Why, yes, most assuredly," Margaret responded. "There will be the guest list to draw up, and the invitations to send and the replies to manage, and the menu, and the music, and the food to order..." she trailed off, but the list continued in her head, with a seemingly endless list of tasks that had to be accomplished before the day after tomorrow.

Mrs. Nettle threw her a sympathetic look. "I shall help you, of course, Your Grace."

Jasper chuckled, shaking his head. "It appears you are beginning to comprehend the extent of the toil entailed in this endeavour, are you not? I daresay you may be experiencing a twinge of regret for embarking upon this venture."

Margaret met his eye, and grinned impishly. "Actually, I relish the challenge."

It was meant as a jest, or half of one, or perhaps just a witty remark, but Jasper did not smile. Instead, he flushed, dropping her gaze and looking away.

"You would do well to commence forthwith," he said curtly. "Now, if you ladies would be so kind, I have a considerable amount of work to attend to."

***

The sound of rattling carriage wheels echoed down the drive. They were coming, then.

Heart thumping, Margaret hurried to the window of the front parlour, peering out. She could see a shadowy line of carriages making their slow way up the driveway towards the house, lanterns bobbing on the sides.

Everything was ready, of course. The ballroom was prepared, the floors polished to a high shine and garlands draped everywhere, lit by countless candles. The musicians had been placed on a low platform to the side of the dance floor, tuning up their instruments in preparation for the dancing. There was a refreshment table, as well as punch, champagne, and wine for later. There'd be supper, of course, and Margaret could recite the menu in her sleep.

Goldie looked extraordinary. This wasn't her *official* come-out, of course, but everybody here would know that she was coming out soon. Her gown wasn't as spectacular as her first official ballgown would be, but it was still beautiful. Margaret had chosen a white gown with a sheen of gold fabric over it, cut in a simple and somewhat old-fashioned style, but in a way that undoubtedly flattered her. Her hair had been done simply, swept up and studded with countless tiny gold flowers.

Margaret's gown was a little less showy – tonight wasn't about her, after all – but she'd chosen a burgundy gown with rich lace at the sleeves and neckline, which was cut a little lower than she would have chosen. The bodice was tight, too, nipping in her waist, but there hadn't been time to get it adjusted.

Goldie was standing behind Margaret, picking at the sides of her nails, pale with nerves.

"They're coming?" Goldie whispered. "Margaret, I can't do it. I can't."

"You can," Margaret assured her, coming forward to take her sister's hands. "You can, and you will. Besides, I'll be here this whole time."

Goldie bit her lip. "Aren't you nervous, then?"

Margaret was intensely nervous. She'd hardly slept the previous night and couldn't help thinking of what could go wrong. This was her first gathering as a hostess. And not just any hostess – she was now Her Grace, the Duchess of Stonehaven. People were going to *notice* her.

The first carriage rolled to a stop outside, she could hear the crunching of gravel, and the sound of the footmen's shoes as they hurried to appear at the door and take the coats and shawls. A murmur of conversation reached Margaret's ears, unfamiliar voices that she did not recognize. She squeezed her eyes closed.

"I'm not nervous, Goldie," she heard herself say. "So don't worry about a thing, because *I* am not worried. Everything will be all right, I promise."

Goldie nodded, and reached out to take Margaret's hand. Together, they turned to the doorway, where a tall, well-dressed woman was approaching, a man in a satin doublet walking beside her.

The tall woman smiled, her eyes crinkling up.

"I am Lady Rushford," she said, extending a hand. "I daresay you don't know any of us yet, on account of just moving into the area. I was glad to receive your invite – I don't think any of us have ever visited the Duke recently."

"It's a pleasure to meet you, Lady Rushford," Margaret said, with a rush of relief. "His Grace, my husband, is not yet in attendance, but I am certain he shall arrive momentarily. To be candid, I must confess that I am unacquainted with many of my guests this evening. I acknowledge that this may seem rather remiss, yet I had hoped to become better acquainted with you all tonight."

Lady Rushford chuckled. "And so you shall. I shall stick by your side, if you like, and introduce you to everyone. We're all keen to know the Duchess, of course! And this must be Miss Marigold Molyneaux, if I'm not mistaken?"

Margaret blinked at her. "Why, yes, she is. How did you know?"

"News travels fast," Lady Rushford said, smiling apologetically. "Gossip flies in the countryside, just as much as in London. This my husband, of course, Lord Rushford."

"It's a pleasure," Lord Rushford said, stepping forward with a smile. He was a benign, friendly-looking man in his middle age, and bowed neatly to them both. "If I may say so, both of you are looking beautiful and elegant, tonight, Your Grace, Miss Molyneaux. Not as beautiful as my own wife, naturally..."

Lady Rushford gave a hoot of laughter and hit him on the arm with her fan. "He's a wretch."

Lord Rushford winked at her. "Miss Molyneaux, I should love to take a place on your dance card. Our son will be arriving soon, and I just know he'll ask you, too."

Goldie flushed and smiled, nodding modestly. Margaret hid a smile. She knew her sister had privately worried about not having anyone to dance with, no matter how much Margaret reassured her.

"However, I daresay your card will get quite full," Lord Rushford added, leaning forward with a conspirational smile, "and I shall sign my name near the end. If you desire to rid yourself of me for the sake of a young, comely gentleman, then do so. I assure you, I shall take no offence."

Goldie laughed aloud at that, and Margaret could almost see her nerves melting away.

"I couldn't do that, Lord Rushford! It's most impolite."

"Ah, that is the benefit of living out in the countryside," Lord Rushford laughed. "We allow these informalities. I must insist you take me off your list if necessary, Miss Molyneaux, in case some young gentleman tries to challenge me to a duel!"

Goldie laughed again, and Margaret allowed herself a long sigh of relief.

It's going to be all right. I'm sure it is.

***

The party was in full swing, and everything was going perfectly.

Margaret gently pushed her way through the crowd, holding a glass of champagne in each hand. One for her, and one for Goldie. Goldie's little crowd of admirers would have to fetch their own champagne.

Margaret's head buzzed with names and faces, but she had a reasonably confident expectation of remembering them all. People were friendly, and eager to meet her and know her in a way she hadn't experienced before.

As Lord Rushford had predicted, Goldie's dance card was full already. He had laughingly given up his own place in favour of his son, who *was* very handsome, and Goldie seemed to like very much already.

It's a success, Margaret thought, not quite able to believe it herself. *My party – my first one – is a resounding success. Everybody is having a good time. And I'll get countless invitations after this, and there shall be more parties, and when Goldie makes her come-out properly, she'll have places to go and people to meet.*

She'll be all right. I haven't failed her.

A laughing male voice which sounded remarkably like Jasper caught Margaret's attention. She flinched, glancing to her left a little too sharply. It *wasn't* him, but she knew that Jasper had descended by now and was mingling with the guests. She'd gotten a glimpse of him, enough to see that he was wearing a green suit with a white waistcoat and an emerald cravat pin glimmering at his throat. He looked remarkably handsome, in fact.

Somebody jostled Margaret, and the champagne slopped over her hand, soaking into one of her gloves. Exclaiming to herself, she pushed her way out of the crowd, finding a quiet corner to set down the glasses and assess the damage.

"I leave you alone for a moment, wife, and here you go spilling your food and drink everywhere," remarked a familiar voice from behind her.

Margaret stiffened, her chest tightening. Not in a bad way, unfortunately. She smoothed the front of her gown before she turned around to face her husband.

"There you are," she remarked archly. "I was starting to think you'd disappeared entirely. Or else you'd lost your nerve and didn't plan to attend the party at all."

Jasper tilted his head to one side, grinning. "Now that *would* be unforgivable. By the way, is this what you consider a small, informal party? The ballroom is full."

Margaret winced. "Things did rather get out of hand. I expected some people to decline, but nobody did, and there were a few notes from locals hinting to be invited. I thought it might offend them if I refused, so here we are."

"Here we are indeed," he chuckled, shaking his head.

"Are you upset? I should have let you know exactly how many people were coming."

Margaret paused, frowning up at him. There was a hint of strain around Jasper's eyes, and a furrow between his brow that hadn't been there before. Perhaps the crowded room was making him more anxious than he would let on. Shuffling a little closer, Margaret glanced up at him.

"We can go somewhere quieter, if you like."

Jasper snorted. "What, and have them say that the Duke of Stonehaven is like a nervy girl, scurrying away to hide from crowds?"

"I'll say that I'm too hot, or something like that, and you're escorting me."

He paused, looking down at her with an unreadable expression. "That's kind of you. Why make yourself look weak to make me strong, though?"

She shrugged. "I don't see it as looking weak. I see it as needing a little break from a crowded, hot, loud ballroom, which is the most natural thing in the world."

He held her eye for a moment longer, then sighed, rolling his shoulders.

"That's kind of you, but I can manage. Everybody is staring at me – I don't often appear in Society. My every move will be scrutinized. If your sister can manage the crowd, and she was so nervous about this, then I can manage it, too. I assure you, I shall be quite well; there is no need for concern on my account."

He cleared his throat, glancing away, and Margaret couldn't help but feel that he was not happy with what he'd said.

"The dancing is starting soon, I believe," he said, changing the subject. "You'll be opening the ball, won't you?"

Margaret blinked up at him. "Well, I hadn't intended to dance."

"Don't you like dancing?"

"I...I do, but that is not the crux of the matter. You are not participating in the dance, and I am uncertain how it would reflect upon me to dance without your presence. It would hardly be fitting for me to commence the ball in your absence."

He tilted his head to one side again, eyeing her curiously. Not for the first time, Margaret found herself wondering what he was thinking. She wasn't likely to find out, of course.

"Why am I not dancing, then?"

She frowned. "I told you that you wouldn't have to. I promised that you would not have to dance, since you were already letting me throw the ball. Don't you recall?"

"I recall you telling me that I did not have to dance, but I never said that I *wouldn't*. I don't mind dancing with you. Once, at least."

On cue, the musicians started up, and there was a general rush of couples to the dance floor.

Jasper smiled down at her, and this time she saw a hint of nervousness in his face. He held out a hand.

She took it.

The two of them pushed their way through the crowd, until people began to realize that it was the Duke and Duchess of Stonehaven coming through, and then they began to move out of the way. It sent a fizzle of excitement down Margaret's spine.

It's me they're getting out of the way for, she thought, hiding a smile. *My husband and me. I matter. We matter.*

They took their places on the dance floor, turning to face each other. Jasper was looking down at Margaret with a strange expression on his face, intent and a little sad.

"It's a waltz," he said, placing a hand on her waist. The warmth of his palm seemed to burn through the fabric of her dress. "I hope you don't mind waltzing."

"I don't mind waltzing," Margaret responded.

Chapter Sixteen

Three Days Later

To My Dear Friend, the Duchess of Stonehaven

My most sincere congratulations on your entrance into our humble local society and once again, felicitations on your recent nuptials! Your new station as the Duchess must indeed be a most esteemed one. As I am yet unwed, I trust I may rely
    upon you to introduce me to some distinguished gentlemen, as the fates would have it!

My family and I, having recently come to the countryside, heard of course about your hugely successful soiree. I was a little surprised not to receive an invitation, on account of our firm and long-standing friendship. However, I am sure my lack of initiation was simply an omission, and I shall not hold it against you.

We are hosting a quiet, informal little party on this coming Friday evening, and would be most honoured if the duke and yourself might join us.

I look forward to your prompt reply, as well as resuming our old friendship.

Your Dearest, Oldest Friend, Lady Alice Bow

P.S. I have it on good authority that neither you nor his Grace have any appointments on the evening of this Friday, so I am sure to receive a positive reply! Do not let me down, dearest Margaret! We have a great deal to catch up on.

Margaret crumpled up the letter and threw it away. She glanced across the breakfast table to where Jasper sat, frowning.

"I don't understand," he said. "She sounds friendly."

"She isn't," Goldie huffed. "Lady Alice is a wretch. She was perfectly horrid to Margaret all through the Season. She used to make a game of stealing friends and prospective suitors away from her."

"It's true," Margaret muttered, shaking her head. "If I was talking to a gentleman, whether I seemed to like him or not, she'd come swooping in and steal them away. She accused me several times of standing on her gown and tearing it, and made me pay for it, too. She never missed an opportunity to humiliate me."

Jasper let out a slow breath. "Well, that's upsetting. Forgive me, but what happened to make her hate you so much? I don't mean to throw accusations around, but surely nobody would be so unkind without *something* of a reason?"

"I thought that myself," Margaret admitted. "I've wracked my brains, but I can't think of anything I might have done to her. I didn't know she was here, but I'm not sure I would have invited her if I'd known anyway."

"Be careful, Margaret," Jasper advised. "As the Duchess of Stonehaven, you'll be held to a much higher standard than other people. You can't be seen to hold to petty jealousies or anything like that."

Margaret pursed her lips. "What does that mean, then? Do I have to accept her invitation?"

Jasper was quiet for a long moment, thinking.

"I think we might have to," he said at last. "She doesn't mention Marigold, so *she* doesn't have to go. But if we refuse for no good reason, it might look a little odd."

Margaret glanced at him, lifting her eyebrows. "And here I thought you didn't care what people thought of you."

"I don't. But I do have a reputation to uphold, and if this woman is as bad as you say, she might make trouble for us."

Margaret glanced across at Goldie, who sighed and shrugged helplessly.

"I think he's right, Margaret. Besides, it's just one evening, isn't it? You're a *duchess* now. It's not as if she can really *do* anything to you. Arrive tardily, take your leave promptly, and thus your obligations shall be fulfilled. I am confident in your ability to manage it."

Margaret said nothing, instead stared down at the looping handwriting. Was it possible for handwriting to seem *smug*? If so, Lady Alice's letter had achieved it.

"You will come, won't you?" she asked, glancing up at Jasper again.

He sighed. "I suppose I'll have to."

"Well, if I'd known you were going to be so graceful about it…"

He shook his head, breaking out into a chuckle. "Enough, enough. I know, I'm an ungrateful wretch. I shall come with you, and I shall even keep my complaining to a minimum."

Margaret smiled back, a warmth spreading through her. It was good to see Jasper smiling *properly*. A proper smile that she had put there.

It wasn't her imagination – they *had* been getting closer over the past few days, what with the lessons in reading and writing and the hours in the library that seemed to fly past. Margaret would be a fool to keep denying that she was attracted to Jasper. That was a good thing, wasn't it? Being attracted to one's husband? If only theirs was a more ordinary marriage.

But it wasn't, and that was the end of it.

Things change, though, she thought to herself, shivering. *Nothing stays the same. There's always a chance. Always.*

"We shall go, then," she said aloud. "I shall write back today. God give me strength for Friday."

"God give us both strength," Jasper remarked, and they shared a shy smile once again.

***

Lady Alice's *quiet, informal little party* turned out to be a musicale. Margaret learned that shortly after stepping in the door, fighting her way through the crush of people to get into the ballroom, which was stacked with chairs and packed with guests.

The Rushfords were not there, which was a disappointment, but there were enough familiar faces for Margaret to feel as though the night wouldn't be an absolute drag. She had some people to talk to, at least.

And, of course, she had Jasper by her side.

A quick glance up at his face revealed that he was pale and grim, clearly not enjoying himself. A gaggle of laughing young gentlemen shouldered past them, knocking into him and jostling Margaret, too. Her glass of champagne slopped over her hand and arm, soaking into her gloves.

"Not again!" she bemoaned, setting the glass down and shaking her hand. "These are new gloves."

"Here, let's find a corner to sort it all out," Jasper said, shooting a poisonous glance in the direction of the disappearing gentlemen. They didn't seem to notice.

They found a corner, and Margaret stripped off the damp glove. Jasper was obliged to stand close, on account of the crowd, and she could smell the sharp, expensive scent of his perfume, rich and earthy. Glancing up, she found him looking down at her, his expression strangely intent.

"I'm sorry," she found herself saying.

He lifted his eyebrows. "Sorry? What for?"

"For... for all of this. For making you come here. You clearly aren't having a good time."

He chuckled. "No, I'm not, but I couldn't let you come alone, could I? Besides, I discovered at our party that I quite like dancing, as a matter of fact."

Margaret shivered. It was a pleasant shiver, and nothing to do with being cold. She'd thought about their dance – their waltz – over and over in the days since the party. Had she ever enjoyed a dance quite so much? She could still feel the warm pressure of Jasper's hand at her waist, the reassuring strength in his hand.

The dance had been over entirely too soon, and she found herself more breathless than she should have been. Jasper looked strange, too, his face flushed.

Then they'd parted, leaving the dance floor for the next dancing couples, and that was that. Still, Margaret treasured a quiet hope that one day soon they'd dance again.

Perhaps they'd be dancing tonight.

"We don't have to wait to dance," she found herself saying. "We can dance at home, if that's what you'd like. Goldie's an excellent pianoforte player, so she can play for us, and we'll dance. Would... would you like that?"

He stared down at her, a tiny frown between his eyebrows. "You really do care about what I would like?"

She tilted her head. "Is that a question? I'm your wife, you know."

"That doesn't mean much. My parents were married, and my father never cared a toss about what my mother wanted. One thing does not necessarily follow the other."

She bit her lip, a little taken aback by this blunt and miserable depiction of home life.

"Well, I do care," she said, lifting up her chin. "I care about you. And I can't help but think, Jasper, that you care about me, too."

He swallowed hard, gaze fixed on her face. "Margaret, I..."

He was cut off by a dramatic flourish of music, a loud, echoing chord played on a pianoforte. They both flinched, turning around to find the source of the music. The crowd surged deeper into the ballroom, and

Margaret caught glimpses of chairs, velvet-lined and gilt, set out in neat rows around a circular platform.

"The musicale's starting," she sighed, pulling on her damp glove again. "We should go."

"Best to get it over with," Jasper said, still watching her closely. "But, Margaret, can we continue this conversation later?"

She smiled up at him. "I'd like that. I'd like that very much."

There was no chance of conversation after that. The crowd was too loud, and there was a constant press of people around them, elbow to elbow, as people hurried to find seats. There weren't enough seats for everybody, and a good number of gawky young gentlemen and unfortunate young ladies were left to stand behind the chairs, leaning against the walls and shifting their weight from foot to foot.

Lady Alice, resplendent in a shockingly expensive-looking pink satin gown, stood on the little platform in front of the chairs, where the pianoforte stood. Her gaze raked the crowd, landing more than once on Margaret.

"I didn't greet her when we arrived," Margaret muttered under her breath to Jasper as they took their seats. "That was a mistake."

"There are so many people here. Surely, she can't be offended?"

"You'd be surprised."

Once everybody was seated, Lady Alice clapped her hands for silence.

"Welcome, all, to our musicale," she announced, smiling benignly around. "What a treat we have for you all! As many of you already know, we have newlyweds in our midst – the Duke and Duchess of Stonehaven! Welcome to them both."

There was the sound of hesitant applause. Margaret wanted to sink into the ground but forced herself to sit upright and keep her expression calm.

Then Lady Alice met her eye, and there was such a look of malice there that Margaret's heart sank.

Something bad is about to happen.

"To start off our musicale," Lady Alice said, smiling sweetly, "we will have our dear Duchess of Stonehaven play a piece for us. Come on up, Your Grace."

There was more applause this time. Margaret felt as though she were fused to the chair. She glanced around, the applause echoing in her head. A few people met her eye and nodded encouragingly.

"I..." she began, glancing at Jasper. He was frowning, but only shrugged.

"It is best to proceed and bring this to a close," he said, sighing.

"No, Jasper, you don't understand. I can't."

In a flash, Lady Alice was at their side, looming over them.

"Come on, Duchess, don't be shy," she laughed, then glanced around at the audience. "Her Grace and I attended the same finishing school; so I know that she is so very modest. Come up and play, Your Grace."

Margaret leapt to her feet, dropping her voice into a hiss.

"Lady Alice, you know I'm a terrible pianoforte player. You never asked me to play. I cannot play."

Lady Alice pouted. "But everybody is expecting it now. They think you're being humble, don't they?"

"I shall not do it."

"Well, I can't *drag* you up to the pianoforte," Lady Alice sighed, voice dropping so that only Margaret could hear. "But then everyone present would depart with the impression that the new Duchess of Stonehaven is an insufferable, haughty little prude, who would not even deign to accommodate her hostess with the simplest of requests. That she wouldn't play the pianoforte at a *musicale*. As your old friend, I would of course be devastated. There would be a great deal of talk about your low origins, and how coming up in the world has made you shockingly unpleasant. You *could* refuse to play, but frankly, I would not recommend it."

Margaret swallowed thickly. She glanced down at Jasper. "Tell her, please. I... I can't."

Jasper blinked between Margaret and Lady Alice, suddenly seeming aware that there were eyes on him, and he was expected to speak.

The room had gone quiet, as it was plain that something was wrong. Since their hostess and the new Duchess were whispering urgently together, people were craning their necks, keen to overhear.

"It might be simplest if you just play, Margaret," Jasper said quietly, avoiding her gaze.

"I cannot!"

"I insist," he shot back, still not meeting her eye. "Just play the piano, Margaret. Get it over with. I'm asking you to do it."

There was a long silence after that. Jasper had spoken more loudly than the two women, and people had heard. They had heard the duke command his new wife to play, and so there would be no getting out of it.

Play she must.

Margaret straightened her spine, meeting Lady Alice's triumphant gaze. She turned and picked her way along the aisle, heading to the pianoforte.

There was no sheet of music on the piano, of course. All the ladies asked to participate would have brought their own or memorized their pieces.

Margaret settled herself onto the cold pianoforte stool, fingers hovering over the keys. There was *one* piece she remembered, or half remembered, and that would have to do.

She began, playing a tentative chord which echoed out in the silent room. The next part required her to run her fingers down an octave or two, but she made a misstep and played a wrong note, jarringly loud. Clenching her teeth, Margaret forced herself to continue, her fingers slow and ungainly. She took a pause of several painful seconds to arrange her fingers into the position for the next chord, and then it sounded wrong and she could not figure out why.

The music unfurled, halting and painfully slow, the notes disjointed and oftentimes incorrect. Margaret inadvertently held the pedal down for an inordinate length of time, causing the notes to blur together until she recollected to lift her foot. She played too loudly and too softly, wrong note after wrong note resounding in the hushed chamber.

She realized an instant too late that she did not remember how the piece ended. Had she been a better player, she might have added in a flourish or a series of chords. Goldie might have done something like that and ended it very nicely.

Instead, Margaret played the last chord she remembered – a wrong note among them – and the sound faded away in the silent room.

One could hear a pin drop, and not in a good way. Margaret dragged her hands off the keys, letting them lie limply in her lap. Her damp glove was itching, driving her mad. There were wet patches left from her glove on the keys which would dry stickily now.

There was a whispering in the audience, and Margaret could not bring herself to look. At last, some kind soul started to clap, and few others joined in. It was scattered applause, painfully quiet, for what was no doubt the worst pianoforte playing they had ever heard.

Swallowing hard, and still not looking at anyone, Margaret rose to her feet and descended from the platform. She intended to go straight to her seat and sit there, silently, until the musicale ended and she could make her escape.

She might have known that Lady Alice wouldn't allow that. The woman stepped in her way, smiling triumphantly.

"Oh, dear," Lady Alice sighed. "That was a little embarrassing. I believe that you played a few wrong notes there, my dear."

Margaret met her eye at last. The whispers were getting louder – some sympathetic, some mocking.

"Get out of my way, Lady Alice."

"How rude," Lady Alice tutted, but stepped aside. She moved up to the platform, clapping her hands for silence again. Margaret hurried to her seat, feeling countless eyes boring into her back.

"Well, thank you, Your Grace, for your... ahem, efforts. Now, next we have a lovely piece played by me, entitled..."

Margaret stopped listening. She reached her seat and sat down with a thump. Jasper grimaced.

"That went worse than I thought," he whispered. "I hadn't realised..."

"I don't think I shall ever forgive you," Margaret responded, staring straight ahead.

"What?"

"You heard me. You didn't stand up for me, and I made an absolute fool of myself. I don't think I shall ever forgive you, Jasper."

Chapter Seventeen

He'd made a mistake, a big one. That much was clear.

The ride home was icily silent. Jasper glanced frequently at his wife in the opposite seat, and said nothing.

She was angled away from him, looking out of the window, chin in her hands.

The party had been in full swing when they left. Nobody else was leaving that early, but Margaret was clearly keen to get away as soon as possible. Jasper was hardly any less eager.

They humiliated her, he thought with a shudder. *That woman, wretched Lady Alice Bow, humiliated her.*

And me? I did nothing. Nothing. I just told her to play and get it over with.

He threw another glance over at Margaret. She was perfectly still, not glancing his way even once. He was sure she wouldn't be able to see much out of the window, not with the darkness outside.

Say something. Say something, you fool.

He cleared his throat, leaning forward. Margaret tore her eyes away from the window, staring blankly at him.

"I'm sorry that it happened that way," Jasper blurted out. "You were humiliated, and it wasn't fair."

She blinked slowly. "Humiliated? I was humiliated? I'm sorry, I hadn't noticed."

He bit his lip. "There's no need to be so sharp about it. If you couldn't play well enough in public, you should have said so."

"I *did* say so," Margaret snarled. "And *you*? What did you say? Nothing! You sat there and let me be embarrassed. You made me look stupid and yourself look weak. You've done a bad job, Jasper, very bad indeed."

"I'm not a mind-reader," he snapped. "I'm sorry I didn't do what you wanted me to do, but there's no changing it now. What do you want me to do? Turn the carriage around, storm in, and demand that Lady Alice apologise?"

She sat back against the seat, pressing the heels of her hands against her eyes. "Now you're just making me sound silly."

"You're making yourself sound silly."

Jasper regretted the words as soon as they'd left his mouth. Margaret looked up at him, gaze unreadable in the dark, and stared for a moment. Silence stretched out, heavy and uncomfortable between them. He wasn't entirely sure what he'd expected from her – shouting, perhaps? Accusations? Insults? A demand for the carriage to stop and a subsequent insistence on walking home, in the dark?

Jasper hoped not. He was sure he'd seen a figure in the garden, after dark, once or twice. It was almost certainly nothing more than one of the servants, leaving on some errand or another, if it wasn't just his imagination. The dark could play tricks on one's eyes.

Still, he couldn't shake the feeling of being *watched* these days. It wasn't pleasant, and it was getting harder and harder to convince himself it was his imagination.

He realized with a start that Margaret wasn't going to say anything. Somehow, that was more painful than any shouting would have been.

They finished their journey in silence.

***

"So, you didn't *really* apologise," John said, narrowing his eyes.

Jasper sighed. "I *did*, I told you."

"No, you said you were sorry it all happened that way, and sorry that you didn't do what she wanted. Neither of those are real apologies."

Jasper let out a growl of irritation, flopping back in his seat.

They were in his study, taking their midday tea, and Jasper had told John everything that had gone on the previous night.

"I *did* want to apologise," Jasper muttered. "I should have taken her side, instead of just telling her to play. But is it really such a large thing? Is it so important?"

John shrugged. "It is to her. She was humiliated by a woman who hates her, and then her husband didn't support her. And then you blamed her for it all, Jasper. Of course she's upset."

Jasper nibbled his lower lip, trying to ignore the feelings of guilt. "Well, when you put it that way, it sounds pretty bad."

"I'm not accusing you or blaming anyone, I'm just trying to tell you the truth."

He sighed. "We're meant to have a writing lesson today. I haven't seen her since last night, and she wasn't at breakfast. Do you think she's avoiding me? My father used to give me the silent treatment if I'd offended him, and I don't know if I can bear it from anyone else."

"If she chooses to sulk, there's not much you can do to set this right," John acknowledged. "But you can *try*, Jasper. Don't forget, this is your home, whereas your wife is still settling in. She's struggling, I can tell, and she probably feels as though she doesn't have many friends. Or any friends, really. You must try and empathize with her. Let her know that you care, and you want to make life better for her. I know…" John broke off uncertainly. "I know this isn't my place to say, but I know that your marriage was – is – a practical one. But that doesn't mean you can't be friends, surely?"

Jasper clenched his jaw, avoiding John's eye. He'd thought a great deal about his marriage lately, about the terms they'd set. About what he wanted, and what Margaret may or may not want. At their own ball, when they'd waltzed together, it had felt so perfect. As if they were *meant* to be together. As if, instead of being married, they were almost meeting for the first time, a spark of interest blooming up between them, ready to blossom into something else entirely.

Something like love.

He closed his eyes momentarily, remembering the helpless, miserable way Margaret had stared at the pianoforte keys. He could still hear titters rising from the audience, along with tuts of disapproval and half-smothered whispers.

"You're right," he heard himself say. "I'll talk to her, and I shall do it today."

John gave a small, satisfied smile. "I knew you'd do the right thing, Jasper. I just knew it."

One hour later, Jasper waited in the library. It was just past the arranged hour for their lesson, the large clock in the corner ticking off the seconds.

They were reading a modern book, a novel, which Margaret had suggested. She'd already read it herself and thought that Jasper might enjoy reading a little more if he *enjoyed* the subject of a book.

Generally, he wasn't a great lover of novels, but this one was… well, it was interesting. The author was a man which Jasper had not heard of. Currer Bell was his name, but Margaret kept saying that it was almost certainly a pseudonym and remained convinced that the author was actually a woman. Either way, the book was thrilling, and Jasper was enjoying it. He had to read slowly, but it wasn't as if he were in any rush.

It *was* getting easier. Jasper didn't ever believe he'd be able to read and write with the smoothness and confidence of others, but he could read better than before. It made a difference. A big difference.

He was considering picking up the book and finishing a chapter when he heard approaching footsteps. Jasper bounced to his feet just as the door opened.

Margaret walked in, and paused, one hand on the doorknob.

"You seem surprised to see me," he heard himself say.

"Yes," she answered. "I didn't think you'd come."

"I didn't think *you'd* come."

She stepped properly inside, closing the door behind her. "Why, did you think I'd sulk?"

"I didn't know what to think. Margaret. I am sorry. I didn't take you seriously, and I didn't listen. You had told me before that you didn't play the pianoforte well, and didn't like playing in public. I didn't think, and I apologise."

She swallowed hard, holding his gaze for a moment.

"Thank you, Jasper, that means a lot to me. And the truth is that I'm sorry, too. I shouldn't have expected you to stand up for me when I can't even stand up for myself. I blamed you, and I shouldn't have."

He shrugged. "I apologised badly."

She gave a short laugh. "I think that both of us came off badly from that interaction. But I'm not upset, Jasper, really."

"I'm glad."

There was a small, awkward pause, before Jasper indicated the seat beside him.

"Care to join me?"

She smiled faintly and moved over to sit. "Thank you. I ordered tea to be brought, by the way. I optimistically ordered for two."

He chuckled. "Thank you. I'm glad we're friends again, and I promise I'll be a better husband in future, if we run into Lady Alice."

"I don't know what it is about her," Margaret sighed, settling a little more comfortably into her seat. "Ever since we were young, I've felt cowed by her. I just know she's watching me and laughing, waiting for me to make a mistake. Sometimes it feels like I'm paralysed."

Jasper pursed his lips. "It's true, she came for you right away, without any provocation. Not that I believed you *would* have provoked her," he added hastily, and Margaret threw back a wry smile.

"I can assure you, I've thought it over again and again. I must have done *something* to offend her, but I can't think what. We were almost friends in finishing school together, but things soured while we were there. I can't think why she doesn't like me anymore."

Jasper tilted his head, watching his wife. There was a fire in the hearth, crackling and snapping, the light playing over her face. She looked remarkably beautiful in that light, and his chest ached, arms twitching to pull her close.

Stop it. Be serious. She wants a friend now. She wants somebody to listen.

"What it was like, at finishing school? Did you have a bad time of it?" he asked. "I only bring it up because I was tormented at school, what with my reading and writing problems."

Margaret sighed. "No, nothing like that. Writing and reading is easy for me, and the rest of the subjects didn't seem hard, either. French, geography, history, arithmetic, all that sort of thing. I could do it easily enough. Deportment lessons and music lessons were something different entirely, but our school was a good one, and I was never badly punished for not learning something. I had plenty of friends, and I was happy there. In fact, some of the girls I knew at school are still my close friends. The ones I didn't see regularly in London would write to me."

Jasper narrowed his eyes. "And the teachers?"

"The teachers liked me. As I said, they were kind to everybody, but I was fairly popular."

"And Lady Alice?"

Margaret frowned. "What do you mean?"

"I mean, was she well-liked at school? Was she clever? Was she popular? Were the teachers fond of her?"

Margaret paused, clearly dredging up the memories. "I... I don't think she was. Nobody was *unkind*, but she was terribly arrogant and a little mean, so people just left her alone. The teachers always seemed exasperated with her, and she struggled with many of the subjects. But you can't imagine *that* is relevant. It was years ago!"

"Some people hold on to those sorts of things," Jasper shrugged, sitting back. "I think we might have gotten to the bottom of why she dislikes you. She was jealous of you and is determined to put you back in your place."

There was a long pause. At last, Margaret gave a huff, shaking her head.

"That can't be true."

"Why not?"

"Because..." she hesitated, shifting uncomfortably, "Because Lady Alice Bow is rich, and beautiful, and very charming. She was good at music and watercolours and has excellent deportment. She has a powerful family, and can have her pick of the eligible gentlemen."

"And yet she is not married," Jasper pointed out. "Perhaps her character puts men off."

"I'm not sure men care."

He snorted. "Take it from me, we do. I think that Lady Alice is *still* jealous of you. She considers herself more beautiful and charming than you, and with more money, and yet people still prefer you. Why else would she try so hard to steal away your friends and potential suitors? She's making a point. The woman bears a grievance so profound that I am astonished her composure does not falter entirely."

Margaret breathed out slowly, shaking her head. "I just can't believe that. It can't possibly be true. Jealous? Of *me*? It's laughable."

Before he could respond, the door opened, and a maid entered bearing the tea tray. They sat in silence for a moment while she set out the things.

Jasper was suddenly aware that his heart was thumping inside his chest, as if it were trying to get out. He felt breathless, although his lungs were certainly working. He felt... oh, he didn't know how he felt, only that it was dizzying and confusing, and he couldn't decide whether he wanted to laugh or cry.

I do believe I'm in love with her, he thought, the realization hitting him like a runaway carriage to the chest. *I love her. Generally, being in love with one's wife is a good thing, but I can't help but feel that it's complicating things for me now. For us.*

I ought to be serious. I ought to concentrate on building up a relationship between us, and keeping Marigold safe.

The maid bobbed a curtsey and left the room, leaving them with a tense silence between them.

"Whatever grudge Lady Alice holds against me," Margaret said, breaking the silence at last, "I can't possibly believe that she *envies* me. Why, she has so many advantages over me. She's beautiful and rich, as I've mentioned before."

"And you are kind and intelligent," Jasper countered. "Perhaps Lady Alice would rather have *your* attributes."

"No, that isn't it. I'm simply..." she broke off as Jasper leaned forward, taking her hand in his.

He wasn't sure what had made him do such a thing. Her hand was warm and soft in his, and he fought the impulse to smooth his thumb across her knuckles. He held her hand loosely, so that she could pull away if she wished it.

She didn't pull away.

"I wish you could see yourself as you truly are, Margaret," he said, voice soft. "You *are* beautiful, and charming, and clever. You think so badly of yourself, and I hate it. You don't stand up to women like Lady Alice because you almost believe they are *right* to think badly of you."

She sighed, shaking her head. "I'm a fool."

"No, you aren't. You are not a fool, Margaret. And I can promise you, here and now, that I won't let this happen again. You're the Duchess of Stonehaven, and you will never be humiliated in public like that again. Or in private. I can swear that to you."

She held his gaze for a long moment, and the air seemed to crackle between them.

"Thank you," she said, voice soft. "That... that means a good deal."

Jasper held her gaze for a long moment, heart pounding.

Margaret was the one to look away first. She gently pulled back her hand, and got up, heading towards the table.

"Well," she said, with false brightness. "Shall we read a little of Jane Eyre's adventures, then?"

Chapter Eighteen

"Excellent teacakes, Lady Rushford," Margaret commented, leaning forward to help herself to another one.

Lady Rushford beamed. "I'm so glad you're enjoying them. And I'm so appalled to hear at what went on at the Bows' musicale the other night! You poor thing. The girl is a terrible host, that's for sure."

Margaret sighed, stirring her tea. "I shouldn't let it get to me, I know. But it *did* upset me. I was just beginning to believe I had established my footing."

She hadn't *meant* to tell Lady Rushford the story about the musicale and her humiliation. It had just come out, bit by bit.

It was time to pay visits, and Margaret had chosen to visit Lady Rushford first, who'd been so kind to them at their soiree. Paying visits by herself was a little terrifying. She would have preferred to have had Goldie at her side, but Goldie wanted to stay and practise her music. Still, it felt good to be able to talk to *someone* about the humiliation she'd received, and have them agree with her.

"What does the duke say?" Lady Rushford asked, eyeing Margaret over the lip of her teacup. "He must have been furious."

"He was," she sighed, "but it is useless to make more of it than is necessary. Raging at Lady Alice won't undo my terrible pianoforte playing."

"She should never have put you in that position."

Margaret shrugged. "She doesn't like me, and she never has. She would have jumped upon the opportunity to make me feel small. And she succeeded."

"Remember this, though, my dear. Nobody can make you feel small against your will. You *always* have control."

Margaret smiled weakly. "Easier said than done."

"Oh, I agree. Still, a good thing to keep in mind," Lady Rushford sipped her tea. "And how about Miss Marigold, how is she?"

"Oh, Goldie is doing well. There's... there's a little unpleasantness between us and our mother. Mama has a suitor in mind for Goldie, but Goldie doesn't like him."

A line appeared between Lady Rushford's brows. "Hm. While I'm all for children listening to their parents, even in matters of the heart, if she *dislikes* the man, that should be the end of it."

Margaret stared down into the amber depths of her tea. She shook her head, speaking almost to herself.

"That should be the end of it. But something's wrong, Lady Rushford, I just know it. Sometimes I wonder if I even know..."

She broke off abruptly at the sound of running footsteps. The door was thrown open without ado, and Lady Rushford leapt to her feet at once.

"What is the meaning of this?" she demanded, but Margaret held out a hand.

"It's James, one of the footmen," she explained. "James, what's wrong?"

"Sorry, Your Grace, your ladyship," the footman said, breathing heavily. "Mrs. Nettle sent me, Your Grace. It's an emergency. You're to come at once. At *once*, she said."

Margaret's heart sank into her stomach. She set her teacup down with a *clack*.

"I'm coming, James. I'm coming at once."

***

Margaret leaned forward, heart thudding. The carriage rattled up the drive faster than it should have done. There was a sense of urgency about James' manner, and he had not explained what had happened beyond claiming that there was a *disturbance*.

Mrs. Nettle, he said, was 'containing it', but Margaret had to come quickly. At once, he'd repeated.

Anxiety fizzled in Margaret's gut, and she quietly prayed that the carriage would go faster.

She heard a shout from up ahead, and a woman's shrill scream.

No, not a woman's, a *girl's*. Goldie's.

Margaret threw open the carriage door before it had even stopped moving, tumbling out onto the gravel below.

A stout, dark carriage stood before the residence, a pair of lean horses hitched to it.

The carriage was evidently a hired conveyance, with two surly, hard-featured drivers lounging in front. The door to the carriage stood ajar, as did the entrance to

the house.

The men came forward, getting between Margaret and the door.

"Stay back, lady," one of them growled. "This doesn't concern you."

"Doesn't concern me?" she spat. "I am the Duchess of Stonehaven. This is my house, and you are trespassing. Get out of my way, or you'll be sorry."

The men hesitated, glancing at each other. They were hired too, no doubt.

"This is a family business," the other man spoke up. "A mother coming to retrieve a wayward daughter. Best to stay out of it, eh?"

Margaret snarled. "That *wayward* daughter is my sister, and she's under my protection. And, might I add, the protection of the Duke of Stonehaven. Do you think you'd like to make an enemy of him?"

The men exchanged brief, worried looks. The implication, clearly, was *no*.

One man grunted unintelligibly, nudging his companion, and they slowly, reluctantly moved aside. Margaret barged past, making a beeline for the stone steps. She was suddenly terrified that she would turn her back for a moment and hear the door of the coach slam closed, and then turn around to see it trundling away, with Goldie trapped inside it.

She knew, without needing to *know*, that her mother was behind this. *It's a new low. Hired men? Black hired coaches? Kidnap?*

The hallway was deserted, but there were signs of a struggle – a smashed vase, a chair knocked over. Margaret clearly heard Goldie's voice from the open parlour door.

"Let *go* of me, Mama! Why won't you listen?"

Lady Keswick's voice came back, harsh and angry. "Why won't *you* listen, girl? You are coming with me, and that's that."

Margaret flung open the door wider and strode inside.

"What's going on here?"

Lady Keswick stood in the middle of the room, her fingers wrapped around Goldie's wrist, pulling hard.

Mrs. Nettle stood beside Goldie, clutching her other arm. Her face relaxed in relief when she saw Margaret.

"Your Grace! You're back, at last," Mrs. Nettle sighed. "Lady Keswick arrived some time ago, shortly after your carriage left. She pushed her way in and began demanding that Miss Marigold pack her things and leave with her. Miss Marigold refused, and then Lady Keswick here began trying to drag her out to the coach."

"She's my daughter," Lady Keswick spat. "Why should I not take her home? I've been patient enough with you, Marigold. Enough is enough. How much further is this supposed to go?"

Goldie shook off her mother's grip and darted over to stand beside Margaret.

"Thank you, Margaret," Goldie whispered, her voice shaking. "You came just in time. It's like she's possessed."

Mrs. Nettle crossed the room, half placing herself between Lady Keswick and the two sisters.

"You have outstayed your welcome, madam," Mrs. Nettle said bluntly. "I think it's time you left."

Lady Keswick glared at her. "You're just a housekeeper. I bet you don't have any children of your own, so why on earth should I listen to you? You have no idea what you're talking about."

Margaret turned her back on her mother, facing Mrs. Nettle.

"Would you call the footmen, please? I'd like a few of the servants around as my mother leaves. There are also two men outside by a coach, hired by my mother. I don't know if they'll cause trouble, but I'd like to be ready just in case."

Mrs. Nettle nodded. She'd paled, Margaret noticed, and took a step closer to whisper.

"I sent the servants away to begin with, as Lady Keswick was making quite a scene. I didn't want them to witness it. I... I didn't imagine that she would try and drag Miss Marigold out. I am to blame for all of this. If the young lady is hurt..."

"I'm not hurt, Mrs. Nettle," Goldie spoke up, her voice a little steadier now. "You were protecting me, I know. Don't feel as though you did something wrong."

"She's right, we're not upset at you," Margaret soothed. "Thank you for your help, and your care of my sister. I don't like to imagine what would have happened if you weren't here."

Mrs. Nettle tightened her lips. "This is something new, Your Grace. We... we can discuss it later, but I believe we are going to have to be more careful in future."

She shot a pointed look at Goldie, and Margaret's chest tightened.

She's in danger. My sister is in danger. What on earth am I meant to do about that?

Mrs. Nettle made a neat curtsey and disappeared out into the hallway.

Silence descended once she was gone, and both sisters turned to face their mother.

"Mama," Margaret said, voice shaking. "What have you done?"

Lady Keswick looked terrible. Her skin was livid and pale, her expression taut. She seemed to have lost weight, and Margaret noticed hollows in her cheeks and dark smudges underneath her eyes. Her hands fluttered constantly, long fingers picking at her skirts, her cuffs, her own skin.

"What I must," Lady Keswick said, her voice just as strong and steady as ever. "I'm fed up with being denied what is mine. Marigold is my daughter, and I will decide what happens to her. You can tell me otherwise as much as you want, but it is my *right*."

"You're lucky my husband isn't home," Margaret snapped. "He'd have thrown you out by your hair."

"Oh, your husband? The grand duke? I know all about him, you know. I know that he's a simple-minded fool that can't even write his name."

Margaret shot across the room, hand raised, before she knew what she was doing. Lady Keswick glanced at her lifted hand and sneered.

"Oh, you raise your hand to your own mother now, do you? How low you have plunged, Margaret."

Margaret brought her hand down, face burning. "I apologise for that, Mama. I should not have done that. But you should not have spoken against my husband. I care for Jasper, and I won't hear you speak about him like that. Besides, he isn't simple-minded."

Lady Keswick gave a huff. "Whatever you say. I'll ask you one last time – will you return Marigold to me?"

Margaret stared at her mother, holding her gaze.

"No, Mama. I won't."

Goldie sidled closer to her sister, clutching her arm as if for support.

"Mama was speaking strangely," she whispered, low enough for only Margaret to hear. "When she was trying to drag me out, she kept saying that she was sorry, that she *had* to do this, that if there was another way, she would have found it. She said that it was my duty, and that I... that I had to save her."

Margaret frowned. "Save her?"

She nodded. "I asked her what she meant, and she told me to hold my tongue. Margaret, she scared me. It's the first time I felt that my mother was gone, and this... this *creature* was in her place."

Margaret turned back to Lady Keswick. "Mama, is there something weighing on your mind? Are you in danger? In debt? Some reason why you feel that Goldie *must* marry Lord Tumnus?"

Lady Keswick raised her chin. "None of your concern."

"It is my concern, when you're breaking into my house, attacking my staff, and trying to kidnap my sister."

"My daughter!"

"She isn't mine or yours, Mama!" Margaret cried out in desperation. "That's what you can't see. Let her live her life, can't you?"

Lady Keswick pressed her lips together, in a thin, bloodless line.

"I wish I could," she murmured, almost too quiet to hear. "I truly wish I could."

Margaret narrowed her eyes. "There's something you aren't telling me. If you'd just tell me, just confide in me, then... well, could I not help you? I *would* help you, Mama. I would."

Lady Keswick stared at her two daughters, emotion warring in her eyes. For one breathless moment, Margaret thought she would agree, and the whole story would come out, whatever it was.

She was wrong. Lady Keswick tilted up her chin, and the cold, vacant look came down over her eyes again.

"This isn't finished, Margaret. I won't stop, you know. I'll never stop."

Without another word, she strode out of the room, pushing past her daughters. Goldie clutched at Margaret as she went by.

"Stay here," Margaret instructed. "I'll make sure she leaves."

Leaving Goldie in the parlour, Margaret hurried after her mother, watching her stride across the courtyard, towards the hired coach.

"Don't come back," she called. Lady Keswick stopped, but did not turn around. "I mean it, Mama. You won't be received here again."

She began to walk on, slowly, and climbed alone into the coach. The two men climbed ungracefully up onto the driver's seat, snapped the reins, and they were off. Margaret stood and watched until the ugly little coach was a blocky shape in the distance, and only then did she go inside.

"The door is to be kept locked," she said, addressing a footman hurrying along the hallway. "Locked, always, do you understand?"

The man bowed and murmured agreement, and Margaret went on into the parlour.

Goldie was sitting on a low footstool, hunched over, and staring into space.

"It wasn't her," she said, as Margaret came in. "That is, it *was* her, but not the woman I recognise. Not my mother. I don't know if I can forgive her for this. Margaret, I... I think I might hate her."

Margaret bit her lip, settling down beside her sister.

"Something is going on, Goldie," she said quietly. "I don't know what, but there is *something*. Mama wasn't always like this, was she? Something's happened, and I bet Lord Tumnus has something to do with it. We'll discover what, and then things will go back to the way they were."

"They won't," Goldie said listlessly. "They never will. Are you going to tell the duke about this?"

Margaret nodded, and Goldie smiled, clearly relieved.

"I'm glad," she continued, leaning against her older sister's shoulder. "He listens to you. He's clever, and I feel as though he cares about me. About both of us." She shot a look at her sister. "He likes you, Margaret. He likes you a lot."

Margaret bit her lip, a frisson of something shooting through her chest. "I... I hope so. We're married."

"Yes, but it's a strange sort of marriage, isn't it? You know, I wouldn't mind having a marriage arranged for me, if it was to be the sort of relationship that you and the duke have. I wouldn't be surprised if you two fell in love, one day."

Margaret's cheeks heated, and she suppressed a shy smile. "I sometimes feel that way, too. But I couldn't ask that of him."

Goldie cocked her to head to one side. "Why not?"

"Well, he didn't agree to that, did he?"

She pursed her lips. "Do you ever think that perhaps he thinks the same about you? That he couldn't ask it of you, when all along you would be happy to give it?"

Margaret could find nothing to say for a moment.

"No," she said at last. "I haven't thought of it that way."

Goldie allowed herself a small smile. "You should. Think about it, I mean."

Chapter Nineteen

Two Days Later

"We don't have to do this, if you don't want to," Jasper said, leaning forward to peer out of the carriage window. "We can turn around and go home right now, if you want."

"That would be cowardly," Margaret responded, staring up at the Bows' fabulous manor house. Today, they were coming in the daylight, so the full grandeur of the place could be fully appreciated.

Frankly, Margaret thought it was ugly.

The invitation was for a garden party, sent by Lady Alice herself. She'd added a mocking postscript promising not to make Margaret play the pianoforte, and that had stung. Lady Rushford had told Margaret that nobody could make her feel small unless she allowed it, but that didn't feel particularly realistic at that moment.

She'd gone all the way over to the fireplace, holding the invitation between finger and thumb, but something made her hesitate. She squinted down at the invitation, inches away from the licking flames, and something hardened inside her.

No. I'm not going to hide away. I'm not a coward. I'm not afraid. *I'm not going to tolerate this treatment any longer.*

So, she'd taken the invitation away from the fire and written out a neat reply, confirming her attendance.

I hope her jaw falls open when she reads it, Margaret had thought, as she wrote. *She looks like a fish when she does that.*

At the time, accepting the invitation felt like something bold and brave, something *strong*. Now that the time had come to actually attend the garden party, she felt a little less courageous. Turning the carriage around and going home *did* feel appealing. After all, Jasper had work to do. They were both working to get to the bottom of Lady Keswick's motivations, as well as the connection between Lord Tumnus and her. They weren't exactly getting any answers, but there were *leads* to follow, surely.

"No," Margaret said, as bravely as she could manage. "I'm going in. You'll stay with me, won't you?"

"Of course. But won't Lady Alice make things difficult for you again?"

Margaret clenched her jaw, tilting up her chin. "She'll try, I'm sure. But I've had enough of her nonsense, and I'd like to put a stop to it now."

Jasper nodded approvingly. "Very dramatic. How are you going to put a stop to it, then?"

"Oh, I haven't thought about that yet. I am hoping something will occur to me."

He winced. "Let us both hope it does. Come, my dear wife. Let us make our entrance."

He climbed out of the carriage first, extending a hand to Margaret. She took it, after only a second's hesitation. His hand was warm and strong, calloused in a way that gentlemen's hands usually weren't. She didn't mind. In fact, she liked it.

"Let us make our entrance," she repeated, and they turned to face their fate together.

The gardens of Bow House were, of course, immaculate, manicured beyond what nature would ever have allowed. There were rolling lawns and pristine patios, ringed by hedges and perfect little flowerbeds. Not a leaf was out of place, and there was not a weed or stray plant to be seen.

Margaret had little affection for the gardens. It seemed as though every wild and natural element had been meticulously excised, pruned away, and replaced with a stony facade. Indeed, such was likely the case.

Jasper held her hand as they made their way towards the other guests, gathered in a large, circular patio around a long table. Lady Alice detached herself from the group and came towards them. Margaret did not miss how her gaze dropped to their interlocked fingers.

"I'm so glad you could attend!" she cooed smoothly.

"Why would I not attend?" Margaret said at once, smiling coolly. "I said we would be here, did I not?"

Lady Alice's smile, to her credit, did not waver. "Of course, of course. Take a seat, please."

They did so, sinking down into seats side by side at the table.

"What now?" Jasper mumbled.

"I don't know. I hadn't thought this far."

They sat in silence at this depressing news.

"I'm a fool," Margaret said at last, but Jasper took her hand.

"You aren't. You're brave. Pray, since we find ourselves in this solitude and conversation is scarce, might we take this opportunity to deliberate on our course of action regarding Lady Keswick?"

Margaret sighed. She'd told Jasper, of course, about Lady Keswick's barging in and attempted kidnapping of Goldie. He'd been suitably grim and serious. There's been no more word from the woman, but Goldie was melancholy and nervy and had slept poorly since the incident. Margaret was worried, and had no idea how things could be changed.

"You ought to talk to your mother," Jasper said at last.

Margaret rolled her eyes at him. "Do you think I haven't tried that? I know something is wrong, but Mama won't explain what. I don't know what to do."

He bit his lip, considering. "I've heard rumours. Not solid facts, just gossip, you understand."

The hairs on the back of her neck prickled. "And what rumours are these?"

He sighed. "Rumours of debts. Serious ones. Whether debts of her own or debts incurred after I paid off your estate, I couldn't say. But I believe she's afraid of something."

"Or someone," Margaret said grimly.

Lady Alice Bow crossed the front of the table, shooting a quick, calculating look at Margaret. It was an unfamiliar look, and Margaret frowned. Lady Alice pulled out a pocket watch, checked the time, and walked on, never once looking back.

A sense of unease settled in Margaret's gut and refused to dissipate.

"Something's wrong," she breathed.

"Hm?" Jasper asked, in the middle of sipping a cup of tea.

"I'll... I'll be back soon," she murmured, then got up from the table.

Lady Alice headed towards the house, slipping inside, checking the pocket watch again.

"Lady Alice," Margaret called, and had the satisfaction of seeing the woman jump almost out of her skin. She spun around, recovering her composure quickly enough.

"Your Grace!" Lady Alice laughed. "Whatever are you coming inside for? The party is out there."

"I wanted to talk to you," Margaret said, coming within arm's reach from the woman. Lady Alice eyed her warily.

Why the wariness? And why does she keep checking the time?

"I wanted to talk to you about what happened at your musicale," Margaret said, keeping her voice even. "When you forced me to play in front of everyone."

Lady Alice barely suppressed a spiteful smile. "How did it feel, then, to feel like a fool in front of everyone?"

"I don't understand. Did you do it deliberately?"

Lady Alice sighed, tossing her hair over her shoulder. "Perhaps I did, perhaps I didn't. I really can't recall. It's not my fault you were so bad at the pianoforte. I ought to have remembered, on account of how badly you played at finishing school."

Margaret swallowed down her outrage and took a step forward. It was somewhat gratifying to see Lady Alice take a step back.

"You asked me how it felt to feel like a fool in front of everyone. Why did you want me to feel that why? Why do you pursue me in this manner?"

A heavy silence enveloped them. It dawned upon Margaret that Lady Alice remained oblivious to the truth. How could she possibly grasp it? She had entombed her grievances beneath years of denial and ire, repeatedly, much like a fragment of shattered porcelain interred beneath the soil, long since obscured from view.

"Because I felt like such a simpleton beside you," Lady Alice said at last, shrugging. "They all loved you at school. It was effortless for you."

"You... you weren't a simpleton."

"No, of course not," she snapped, taking a step forward. "But I *felt* like one. I felt like a fool, when all along I was better than you."

"We were *children*," Margaret insisted. "Nobody was better than anybody else. Is this truly why you've resented me for all this time?"

Lady Alice sneered. "Oh, look at you, such a little saint. *You* would never hold a grudge. You're so very ordinary, plodding through Society without looks or money, and yet here you are, married to a duke. It's so ridiculous. The world has been turned upon its axis, and if I must humble you a notch or two to rectify it, Your Grace, I shall not hesitate to do so."

Margaret gave an incredulous, mirthless laugh. "You think I *wanted* this? I never chose my marriage."

Lady Alice curled her lip. "Oh, don't be a little fool. You adore him, I can see it in your eyes when you look at him. And he adores you, foolish that he is. And you don't even know how to behave as a duchess! For what it's worth, any duchess of any breeding would *know* that she would be expected to play at a musicale like that. But no, you weren't prepared and brought shame on your name without even *trying*. Really, it's remarkable."

Margaret had not heard the majority of the last part of this speech.

"I don't adore him," she managed, which was probably not the best thing to say to a woman like Lady Alice.

Do I... Do I look at him like that? Adoringly? And how does he look at me? I never thought I'd seen anything like that in his eyes.

Could it be true? Could I have learned the truth from Lady Alice Bow, of all people?

Swallowing hard, she put the thought aside. Now was certainly not the time, and Lady Alice was *not* the person to have this discussion with.

"I don't want to be enemies," she said at last. "I'm fed up with all of this. We don't have to be friends, Lady Alice, but I can't let you treat me this way. Why don't we just leave it all behind us, and move on? I want a quiet life."

Lady Alice eyed her with open distaste. "And if I don't agree, you'll bring your big, powerful husband to scare me, will you not?"

Margaret looked her in the eyes. "No, Lady Alice. I don't need others to fight my battles for me."

She snorted. "Fighting what battles? Is that a *threat*, my dear?"

"A threat? No. But should you attempt to humiliate me in public in such a manner again, I shall be compelled to behave in such a manner that your teeth shall rattle out of fear. That, I assure you, is a most earnest threat. There's a difference, don't you think?"

Lady Alice blanched and took a step forward. "Why, you ought to..."

She broke off abruptly, reaching in her pocket for the watch. Margaret watched, baffled, as she flipped it open, checking the time. A slow, smug smile spread over her face, and a cold feeling trickled down her spine.

"You're too late," Lady Alice breathed, breaking into a chuckle.

Margaret swallowed hard. Her throat was suddenly dry. "Too late? Too late for what?"

Lady Alice eyed her thoughtfully, then dug into her pocket, withdrawing a crisp, folded note.

"This arrived for me this morning," she said smoothly. "Read it. Go on."

Margaret unfolded it, and her heart sank at once. It was a simple and brief note, but she felt more and more panicked with each word.

To my Dear Lady Alice Bow,

I should be much obliged if, when my daughter Margaret arrives at your garden party today, you would be able to keep her there until at least half-past two. After that hour, it does not matter if she stays or goes – it will be entirely too late.

I know that you have often thought that my daughter requires humbling, and I am afraid I must agree. I hope you'll help me in this and speak not a word of it until after the business is completed. It will be for the best, in the end.

I am obliged for your help.

Your Friend, Lady K.

"Lady Keswick," Margaret whispered unnecessarily. "She wrote to you. Why? What... what is all this?"

"I don't know what she meant," Lady Alice said, shrugging. She snatched back the paper, folding it neatly and sliding it into her pocket again. Crossing her arms across her chest, she eyed Margaret with unmistakeable triumph. "I wonder if it has something to do with your sister, Marigold? Oh, dear."

Wordlessly, Margaret turned on her heel and began to stride away along the hallway. She heard Lady Alice scurry after her.

"Don't walk away from me, you wretch! I haven't finished. You are entirely above yourself, duchess, or not, and I... stop walking away!"

She grabbed at Margaret's arm, hauling her around to face her. Margaret tugged her arm free, teeth clenched.

"Get off me! Jasper was right. I can't believe it. You *are* jealous of me. Of me!"

Lady Alice blanched. Pray, Lady Alice, I cannot help but feel a measure of pity for you, and I would never wish to find myself in your position. It is a lamentable existence, to derive pleasure from the lives of others rather than embracing one's own. I must implore you, do not entertain the notion of addressing me again, for your heart, alas, is far beneath mine.

Turning on her heel, she strode out into the sunlight, making a beeline for the table. Jasper still sat there, looking thoroughly bored. As she approached, he smothered a yawn.

"Jasper," she hissed urgently. "Jasper, how many of the servants are at home today?"

Jasper paused, frowning. "Well, let me see. It's market day, so the cook and some of the kitchen staff will be shopping. A few of the footmen have the day off, and... oh, it's Mrs. Nettle's half day off."

Margaret went cold. "Mrs. Nettle isn't in the house?"

Jasper eyed her, frowning. "Something's wrong, I know it. Why should it matter if Mrs. Nettle isn't at home?"

"Because we aren't at home," Margaret responded, icy fear stroking down her spine. "The three of us are Goldie's protectors. She's almost alone in that house, and vulnerable."

"But so long as she doesn't go outside..." Jasper began, but he spoke half-heartedly. She could see the fear in his face, too.

"We have to go home," Margaret said, voice shaking. "We have to go home right now."

"I'll call for the carriage," Jasper said, rising to his feet at once.

Margaret swallowed, closing her eyes, and recalled what Lady Alice had said.

"Jasper, I think it may already be too late."

Chapter Twenty

"You don't think it's a little late for a walk, Miss Marigold?" Janey Nettle asked, raising an eyebrow. "It is not dark yet but quite late for a walk don't you think?'

Marigold sighed and yawned, stretching her arms above her head. "I don't want to spend the whole day just sitting down. I thought just a small walk would be nice."

Janey nodded and said nothing. Now, Janey Nettle had had her fair share of troublesome charges to watch over – when he was young, managing Jasper had been no picnic, to say nothing of his wretched parents – so she knew how to manage it. However, her skills were all but useless here; Miss Marigold was really a breath of fresh air. It was clear the girl was lonely, with her sister gone out for the afternoon, and so Janey had allowed her to trail along from room to room, talking and passing the time. She was a sweet girl, really.

Janey picked up another linen, folding it neatly and adding it to the ever-growing pile. To avoid Miss Marigold wandering between chilly rooms and being exposed to drafts, Janey had brought her remaining work to one of the parlours, where a fire crackled in the grate and there were comfortable chairs. Miss Marigold was sprawled in one at that moment, legs stretched out in front of the fender.

"Wouldn't you rather stay inside, where it's nice and warm?" Janey tried. "It's safe here."

"What danger would there be in the grounds?" Miss Marigold objected. "And you'll come with me, won't you?"

Janey shot her a fond smile. "If you like, of course I'll come."

"I know it's silly, but I feel so on edge when Margaret is away," Miss Marigold sighed, sinking deeper into her seat. "I miss her so much. I suppose it won't do to be so attached to my sister, not now that she's married."

"Nonsense. You two are very close, and her Grace is just as fond of you as you are of her, I can promise you. Now, if you intend to go for a walk, we should leave soon, before it gets late and dark."

"All right," Miss Marigold said, looking a little brighter. It had occurred to Janey before that the girl *did* look a little peaky. It was never good to keep a young, bright girl inside the house all day. Surely a quick walk would do no harm.

They dressed quickly for the weather outside, throwing on shawls and pulling on stout boots. Miss Marigold was humming to herself under her breath, and Janey allowed herself a small smile. It was a pleasure to have young people in the house again, and their presence had done more good for the duke than he would likely ever know.

No, Janey, that's not fair, she scolded herself. *Of course the duke knows how much good it's done to him, having them here.*

He's a married man now. That changes a person. And if love should follow – well, who's to say how things might progress?

She kept these thoughts to herself, however, only offering Miss Marigold an arm. The girl took it, and the two of them stepped out into the nice but cold day.

They walked briskly away from the house, following the wide, stony path which snaked through the trees and ultimately led across the grounds and to the road at the bottom. It would be the route the duke and duchess took when they came home, and Janey couldn't help but wonder whether Miss Marigold was considering this.

For a while, they walked in comfortable silence, and Janey would have been happy enough to leave it that way. It was Miss Marigold who broke the silence first.

"Do you think I'm a bad daughter, Mrs. Nettle?" she asked abruptly.

Janey blinked, startled. "A bad daughter? I should say not."

"My mother was always a good one, you know. I don't want you to think that she was some fairy-tale villain, always wanting to make us miserable, and always formulating schemes. She was usually fairly pleasant. Not perfect, of course, but then, none of us *are.*" Miss Marigold threw a quick glance at Janey. "But if one's parent asks for a thing, aren't we obliged to obey?"

"That depends on the thing," Janey answered staunchly. "My parents wanted me to stop reading so much, and I simply couldn't do that. They wanted me to marry a man I didn't love, and I couldn't do that either. We must love and respect our parents, of course, but not at the extent of sacrificing our own lives. No good parent would want that. Besides, respect must be earned, mustn't it? It isn't worth much if it's just freely given, is it?"

Miss Marigold considered this for a moment.

"I suppose you're right," she said at last. "But that's not what Mama said."

No, I bet it isn't, Janey thought. Aloud, she said, "You're getting older, Miss Marigold, and you'll need to make your own decisions soon enough. Weigh up the advice you're given and think it over long and hard before you make a choice. Especially one regarding *marriage,* because it will affect your entire life, and is irreversible."

There was more silence after this, and Janey wondered uneasily if she had gone too far. Then, to her surprise, Miss Marigold stopped, turning to face her.

"I think, so far, you have given me the best advice out of everyone," she said, voice wobbling. "I know I can't go home, and I know that Mama is not acting in my best interests at the moment. It's just so *hard*. Nobody told me it would be so hard."

Janey hesitated. It was not, of course, her place, but she found that her arms were going out to embrace Miss Marigold before she could stop herself. The girl drooped forward, resting her cheek on Janey's shoulder, and sniffled miserably.

"I would say that I want things to go back to the way they were," she said, "but I wasn't happy then, either."

"Oh, hush, child," Janey murmured. "You're young. Life has a way of working out, you'll see. I promise."

Miss Marigold pulled back, eyes misty and eyelashes wet. She sniffled again, smiling faintly.

"Thank you, Mrs. Nettle. Do you have a handkerchief?"

"Of course," Janey assured her, and began rummaging in her pockets. She was still busy in her search when Miss Marigold spoke again.

"Oh, are they back already?"

"I shouldn't have thought so," Janey responded, pulling her nicest handkerchief out of her sleeve.

"Well, whose carriage is that, then?"

Janey flinched, a sensation of foreboding sliding down her spine. She glanced up and saw that Miss Marigold was staring down the roadway, a frown between her brows. A black, carriage was hurtling towards them, the horses sweating and labouring.

A chill of apprehension settled in Janey's stomach, a sensation of foreboding. She
composed herself and cleared her throat.

"Miss Marigold," she said, voice cracking, "you had better run."

The girl only stared at her, eyes wide. "I... I don't understand."

Janey whirled around to face her. "*Run*, I say! They're here for *you!*"

There was no time to worry about the wisdom of shouting at the Duchess's sister. Miss Marigold, at least, did not object, finally understanding the urgency.

The two of them turned and fled back up the path, gravel skittering under their boots. Janey privately cursed the distance they had walked, putting them close to a quarter of a mile from the house. None of the other servants were visible, nobody to whom she could call for help.

The carriage bore down on them, the horses sweating and neighing. Janey risked a quick glance over her shoulder and saw that there were no less than three men – two in the driving seat, and one hanging out of the window.

We aren't going to make it, she thought, still running blindly.

Then the carriage was upon them, pulling up alongside with a spray of gravel, and two of the men leapt down, the third staying to keep the horses ready. One man snatched up Miss Marigold, lifting her easily off her feet, even while she screamed and fought.

Janey threw herself at him, but the other man shoved her aside, striking her an almost casual blow around the face. It was enough to send her spinning to the ground, the edges of her vision blurring.

You really do see stars, she thought dizzily, trying and failing to pull herself to her feet. Janey had never been struck, not as hard as that, and she had always imagined one could shake it off.

She was wrong. Her mouth tasted of copper, her ears rang, and her balance appeared to have deserted her entirely. She managed to push herself up onto all fours and twisted back to see what was happening to Miss Marigold.

She was just in time to watch one of the men throw a burlap sack over her head and toss her bodily into the carriage. The man climbed in after her, leaving the second to hesitate with one foot on the step.

"What about the older woman?" he said, apparently addressing his question to someone inside the carriage. "Do we need her, too?"

"No," came a familiar, female voice. "Just the girl. Now, quickly! We haven't much time."

"Wait," Janey managed, her voice reduced to a croak. "Marigold, wait!"

The door slammed, with nobody taking any notice of her. The carriage wheeled unsteadily around, narrowly missing running Janey over with one of its vast wheels. It set off at the same rapid pace, leaving her behind. She lifted a shaking hand to her forehead, where it had hit the gravel, and found a sticky matt of blood there. Nothing dangerous, but enough to make her head swim.

By the time Janey was able to force herself to her seat, heart pounding and stomach threatening to throw up her luncheon, the carriage was little more than a black square in the distance. She stumbled after it for a few paces before realising that this was useless, and then turned and began to limp up towards the house.

"Help," she called, although she knew fine well there would be no help to be had, not until she was closer. "Somebody, help. They've taken the girl."

***

When the Duchess arrived, Janey saw at once that she knew something was wrong. In fact, less than fifteen minutes after the kidnapping – after Janey had found help, and explained the situation, and had her head wound tended to by a solicitous footman – the ducal carriage appeared in the distance.

Brushing aside the footman, Janey went limping out to greet the carriage. the Duchess descended first, face ashen and lips pressed into a thin line. She glanced around, no doubt looking for Miss Marigold, and only looked more miserable when she did not see her."

"You got my message already, then, Your Grace?" Janey managed, coming forward. "I sent it about ten minutes ago, I would not have thought..."

"I didn't get your message," the Duchess responded. "I... I learned something at the party which... which rather shook me. I thought that perhaps there might be some danger here, some trouble. And judging by that rather nasty cut on your brow, Mrs. Nettle, I would guess that I am right."

Janey swallowed hard. "I'm afraid the situation is bad, Your Grace."

The duke climbed out of the carriage behind his wife, eyes sharp and alert. He saw Janey, and at once his eyes widened in concern.

"A physician must be fetched," he said at once, "That's a nasty cut, Janey. Perhaps we could go for..."

"I am fine, Your Grace," Janey said firmly. "It's just a cut. I'm a little bruised and shaken, but unharmed. As you might guess, there is something more serious to consider."

The Duchess closed her eyes. "Goldie."

Janey dropped her gaze, not quite ready to look them in the eyes.

"I failed you, Your Graces," she said, voice wobbling. "Miss Marigold and I went for a walk. She wanted the air, and I, foolishly, did not say no. A carriage came up the drive, quite suddenly, and we could not escape it. They knocked me down and bundled her into the carriage, and then they were off."

The duke's face grew grimmer and grimmer as she spoke.

"I see," he said at last. "And were there any distinguishing marks, anyone you recognised?"

"They were masked, with cloths over their faces," Janey recounted grimly. "I don't believe I knew them, and I doubt I could see them again. But I distinctly heard a voice when Miss Marigold was bundled into the carriage, and that I *did* recognise."

The duke lifted his eyebrows. "Well? Come on, Janey, who was it?"

Janey hesitated, just for an instant. It was not a pleasant thing she had to say, but she had a feeling it would not surprise anyone.

"It was my mother, Jasper," the Duchess said, voice heavy and tired. "My mother finally succeeded in kidnapping her own daughter. If they leave town, no doubt they will find a priest who will not object to Goldie's reluctance and marry her with only her mother's consent. Even if Goldie could escape, she has no money and no experience. I'm sure my mother will ensure that she is taken somewhere she has no friends nor anyone likely to help her, either. Once she's married, she's bound to Lord Tumnus, and then who only knows what will become of her. I doubt we'd find grounds for annulment, not with her mother's consent."

The duke muttered a curse, raking his hand through his hair. "So, what now? Do we summon a magistrate, find some constables, set up a search? She could be anywhere. How long ago did this happen, Janey?"

"Not long," Janey answered. "Fifteen minutes, I think. I... I was rather disoriented after the blow and may have lost more time than I thought. I am sorry, Your Graces. I'll never forgive myself."

The Duchess laid a hand on Janey's arm.

"You have done nothing wrong," she said fiercely. "Please, do not blame yourself. You did what you could, and you are *not* to blame for what my mother has done. Jasper, I need you to summon some constables and find a magistrate. In the meantime, I'll try and delay my mother. If I can stop her leaving town, then we may yet have a chance of saving Goldie. Janey, you're to stay here and rest. You've hurt yourself, and you *will* see the physician, I insist upon it. And thank you for protecting my sister."

Janey inclined her head, giving a small smile. Truthfully, her head pounded and she longed to rest, just to stop talking and sip on tea or something like that.

"What are you saying, Margaret? How are we to find them?" Jasper said, frowning. "And what if I arrive too late to help you?"

"Don't worry about that," the Duchess said, throwing a quick, shy smile up at her husband. "And don't worry about finding them – there is really only one place my mother could have gone. I know where to find my sister."

Chapter Twenty-One

Margaret went home. Of course, she did.

Jasper had complained more about being sent off to fetch the constables and whatever help could be found, but Margaret had pointed out that she might well arrive too late, or be unable to gain entry into the place, and then both of their time would be wasted.

This was a valid point, and James did not argue much more.

Not wanting to waste a minute more in debate, Margaret headed straight for the carriage-house, where one of their vehicles was being readied. She had decided not to take any men, as she had a feeling that Lord Tumnus and *his* hired men would be waiting to guard their prize, and she did not want any of the footmen or manservants to be hurt.

It was a reconnaissance mission, nothing more.

"Just... just be careful, won't you?" he murmured, as Margaret turned towards their smallest carriage, neat and nondescript and unlikely to attract attention. She paused, hearing something in his voice that had not been there before and glanced over her shoulder.

Jasper's face was tight, and he smiled faintly when she met his eye.

"I'm just beginning to like you, Duchess," he said. "I'd be upset if I had to go out and find another wife. It's entirely too much trouble."

She lifted an eyebrow. "Was that a *jest*? From the most illustriously serious Duke of Stonehaven? The Beastly Duke himself? Surely not."

He gave a wry smile, shifting his weight from foot to foot. "Before you go, Margaret, I... I would like to talk to you."

She fidgeted with the folds of her cloak – a dark, nondescript thing, hanging heavily around her, with a large hood which could be pulled up to cover her head entirely – and cleared her throat, not entirely sure what to say.

"You are already talking to me."

He rolled his eyes. "Be serious, Margaret."

"I'm sorry, I'm sorry, I just....I need to go, Jasper, I need to go *now*. I promised my sister she'd be safe here. I promised her that *I* would keep her safe, and now she's been snatched away from under my own nose. If our mother has resorted to kidnapping her own child, I really don't know what else she will stoop to. Besides, I know how this story plays out, if Goldie is not rescued."

"The sacrificial lamb," Jasper said, nodding grimly. "She'll marry Lord Tumnus."

"Yes, she'll be forced to. We may already be too late."

He took a step forward, hesitantly taking her hand in his. She sucked in a breath, the sudden contact sending shivers along her skin. Not unpleasant shivers. Margaret's skin prickled with a delicate shiver, concealed beneath the folds of her cloak.

"Ours has been a strange relationship so far, don't you think?" he managed at last, sounding strained. "There are a hundred things I want to say to you, Margaret, but I can't make myself speak them at the moment. I'm not sure I'd have time, not now. But at least let me tell you one thing. I'm glad I married you, Margaret."

She jolted, gaze shooting up to meet his eye. He was looking at her, his expression intent and serious.

"I... I'm glad I married you, too," she stammered, not entirely sure what to say. The familiar warm feeling in her chest was back, but for once, Margaret could not think of a witty retort, or anything clever at all, in fact. "I think we get on well together, you and I. We're friends."

Jasper gave a small, sad smile. "Friends. Indeed, we said we'd be friends, didn't we?"

She'd said something wrong, Margaret was sure of it, but couldn't quite decide what, or how. Before she could think of a way to remedy the situation, or say something else, Jasper let go of her hand, and the spell was broken.

They moved aside, she towards the carriage door, and he towards the entrance of the carriage-house.

"Remember what I said," Jasper said briskly. "Be careful. Be watchful. Do what you can to save Marigold, but please don't put yourself in danger. You see, I... I can't quite fathom what I'd do if I lost you, my dear."

Her heart hitched in her chest. Margaret thought that she could have stayed there forever, her cloak billowing around her and her foot propped up on the step into the carriage, looking back at the man she'd married.

But Marigold did not have forever. She might not even have another half an hour.

"Thank you," she said, her voice a little strained. "Thank you, Jasper. That means a great deal to me."

He gave a short nod, and turned his back before Margaret could climb up into the carriage. She did so at once, of course, and the door was closed behind her. The carriage rattled out of the door and into the growing twilight.

It would be dark soon.

***

Keswick House was almost entirely shrouded in darkness.

Almost.

Margaret knew all the tricks. The debt-collectors would come at this time of day, at twilight, when they would see lit windows and know that the family was home. So, they had three choices – to sit in darkness for hours, to go to bed early, or to learn to barricade the windows well enough so that no light escaped.

Creeping closer, Margaret saw that the crack in the front-parlour shutter was still there, revealing the thinnest, tiniest sliver of light. Coming closer still, picking her way through the dark, overgrown front garden of her old home, she put her eye to the crack and peered inside.

Inside, she caught glimpses of movement. It was Lady Keswick herself, pacing back and forth. No, not pacing, packing. She had a bag open on a sofa and was filling it with books and papers and little ornaments, her face set and determined.

If Mama is here, then so is Goldie, Margaret thought, in a rush. This thought was quickly followed by another. *They're packing. They're leaving, and we are running out of time.*

I can't wait for Jasper.

Backing away, Margaret forced herself to be calm, to *think*.

I can get into the house. The birch beside the window into my old room is easy enough to climb. The lock on my window was broken, so I can climb in. There are few lights on in the house, so I can creep about in the darkness and find Goldie. Then we'll go out the same way, and Mama will never know what happened.

I can't leave her alone with them.

Decided, Margaret hurried back to the carriage, parked a little distance down the street so as not to give them away by the rattle of wheels on cobbles. She gave the driver instructions to return, inform the duke of where she was and what was happening, and come back again to hopefully collect Margaret and her sister.

The driver looked dubious. "This seems a bit dangerous, Your Grace. How are you going to get in?"

"I'll climb a tree."

"W-Would his Grace approve of that?"

She fixed the man with a baleful stare. "If his Grace disapproves, he can take it up with me when he sees me next. In the meantime, *I* am the Duchess, and you'll do as I say."

The driver sighed. "Right you are, Your Grace. I hope you know what you're doing."

"So do I," Margaret muttered, but not loud enough for the man to hear.

***

The birch tree was proved rather more challenging to ascend, given the ample drapery of her skirts and cloak that enveloped her. Margaret nearly lost her footing on more than one occasion, the tree slick with dew and sap, her garments becoming ensnared upon the branches as she ventured higher. At one point, her shoe slipped and she lost her footing entirely, finding herself dangling by her hands. She recovered, hauling herself slowly upwards, inch by inch.

At long last, Margaret found herself astride the thick branch which stretched out opposite her old bedroom window. She was perspiring heavily, her hair coming undone, covered in a dozen scratches, but she was *here*.

Please let it not be blocked, she prayed and reached over to open the window.

It slid open, and Margaret's heart leapt. Getting *inside* the room was a little trickier, trying to convey herself *off* the branch and *onto* the windowsill without either toppling to the ground below or landing on her bedroom floor with a *thump*.

For Goldie, she reminded herself, every time she felt as though she would fall, heart pounding and sweat trickling down her temples. *You can do this for Goldie.*

When she carefully stepped down onto her bedroom floor, it felt like a small victory.

Now what?

She turned, intending to head purposefully towards the door. A shadow shifted in the corner, and she froze, heart dropping into her stomach.

"Margaret?" came a tiny voice, and a figure rose uncertainly to its feet. "Are you really here?"

Margaret swallowed thickly. "Goldie? You... You're in here?"

The shadow of her sister came lurching forward, limping slightly on one ankle. It *was* Goldie. The moonlight trickled in through the window, illuminating a tear-stained face and dishevelled hair and Margaret felt a sudden urge to find the men who had kidnapped her and punish them.

"Mama kidnapped me, but I suppose you know that already," Goldie said, voice heavy. "They brought me back here. They were going to lock me in my room, but I begged to go into your room. It's silly, I know, but I... I slept in here after you left, before you came to fetch me. I missed you, you see. They won't let me have a candle or a fire."

"It's freezing in here. The cruel wretches," Margaret muttered. She came towards her sister, wrapping her in her arms. "But you're safe now. Well, nearly safe. I came to get you, and Jasper is coming soon with constables and men. We're going to take you away, and after this, nobody will let Mama have you again, I promise you. What's wrong with your ankle?"

"I tried to struggle when they took me, and I twisted my ankle badly," Goldie responded miserably. "I can hardly walk. I won't be able to run, Margaret."

"What about climbing? Can you do that? I assume that door is locked from the outside."

She nodded. "It is locked. I tried banging on it for a while, but of course they ignored me. I don't know if I can climb, but I'll try. I'll go very slowly and be very careful. Besides, it's the only way out, isn't it?"

"That's right," Margaret paused, smiling and ruffling her sister's hair. "You're very brave, you know. It's nearly over, all of this. I know what they planned – to take you away, and hide you, and force you to marry that wretched lord. It's an evil plan."

Goldie hesitated, and Margaret frowned. "Why? What is it? Tell me, Goldie."

"That's not exactly the plan," she murmured. "The... the marriage is to take place here, *before* we leave. Lord Tumnus has gone to fetch the priest who agreed to do the ceremony, and he'll be back any minute. I could hear them talking about it downstairs."

A pang of fear rushed through Margaret. *Another half an hour, and I might have been too late.*

"Then we'd better waste no time," Margaret said firmly. "Come, let's get you out onto the tree outside."

Goldie nodded eagerly, and hobbled urgently towards the window. Her injured ankle twisted and she lurched forward, stumbling. Margaret tried to catch her, but she was just an instant too late. Goldie knocked into a little low table, with a tall vase sitting in the centre.

Margaret knew what was going to happen before it did. Time stretched out, yet she could not move. The vase wobbled, slowly and thoughtfully, as if it were considering whether to fall or not, and then it toppled.

Crash.

Glass shards shot all over the floor, a tremendous noise in the darkness. Margaret heard a stifled gasp from downstairs, and the sound of hurrying feet.

Goldie looked stricken. "I've ruined everything," she gasped, pressing her hands to her mouth.

"It's all right, Goldie, we may be safe yet. If Mama just calls to you through the door, say that everything is fine and you just knocked over the vase. Say that..."

There was no more time for talk. A key clicked in the lock, and the door flew open. A flickering candlestick threw misshapen shadows across the room, and both Margaret and Goldie blinked in the sudden light.

With slow, deliberate steps, Lady Keswick walked into the room, holding up the candle.

"Well," she said at last. "Here you are, Margaret. I can't say I'm surprised."

"No, you can't," Margaret replied, firmly putting herself between her mother and her sister. "Step aside, Mother. I'm here to take Goldie home. I don't wish to hurt you, but if I have to push you aside myself, I will."

Lady Keswick cocked her head, thoughtfully inspecting her oldest daughter.

"You are the most like me, I think," she murmured. "But with none of my *vices*. Not yet, at least."

"Vices?" Margaret echoed, curious despite herself. "What are you talking about?"

Lady Keswick sighed, setting down the candlestick. The light was poor, not enough to illuminate the room properly. It cast unpleasant shadows across Lady Keswick's face, her shadow stretching across the floor towards them.

"You deserve an explanation, I think," Lady Keswick muttered. "When your father died, he left us destitute, as you know. Things were difficult. In desperation, I took to a card-table. I had a rather good run of luck, and ended up earning enough money to pay off one or two pressing debts. I was thrilled; had I finally stumbled upon a way to support us?"

Margaret let out a long sigh. "Can I assume that you did not?"

Lady Keswick shrugged. "I played sparingly, and in fact, rather well. I won money, which served us well for a while. Of course, I began to lose more than I won. These were not quite the same sorts of debts as your father's. He was a gentleman and owed a gentleman's credit and respect. I was just a woman, and a gambling one at that. My creditors were a little more... dangerous. When the Duke of Stonehaven paid off the estate's debts, he of course did not know about mine. I thought I had time. I intended to wait until you were settled into your marriage, and then ask for the money. It would be humiliating, but I was ready to do it." She paused, breathing out. "Then, a few days before your wedding, Lord Tumnus approached me and revealed that he had bought my debts. He intended to charge an extortionate rate of interest. He would cancel them all in exchange for Marigold's hand in marriage."

There was a taut silence.

"You sold your own daughter to pay your debts?" Margaret managed at last. "Why? Why didn't you come to me?"

Lady Keswick gave a bark of laughter. "And endure your pity, your triumph? No, I think not. I had my pride, after all."

"So it was pride, then?" Margaret echoed disbelievingly. "You would sell her for *pride*?"

"I was in too deep!" Lady Keswick snapped, some of her calmness deserting her. "You cannot blame me."

"Oh, yes I can. You've done badly, Mother, very badly indeed."

"You haven't thought of how this would affect you, and *him*," Lady Keswick said, jabbing a finger accusingly at her daughters. "A gambling mother-in-law, chained to the card-tables? He would be humiliated."

"He would not care, I can answer for it." Margaret paused, tilting up her chin. "Anyway, it doesn't matter. You aren't taking Goldie. We're leaving, and there's nothing you can do about it. Unless you have some weapon, or intend to fight me, Mother, you can't keep us here. We're going."

Margaret reached out, taking Goldie's cold hand in hers, and squeezed it.

Lady Keswick moved aside, leaving the doorway exposed. She held out a hand.

"Go on, then. Abandon your mother. Defy her once more. You've already done it so often, why not once more?"

Margaret eyed her mother. There had to be some trick. *Something was up.*

"Let's go, Margaret," Goldie whispered. "Let's *go*."

The two sisters began to inch towards the door, keeping a wary eye on Lady Keswick. When they were level with the older woman, Margaret saw Lady Keswick tilt her head, as if listening for something. Her heart sank.

"Not so fast," came a smug voice, and Lord Tumnus stepped into the doorway. He was grinning widely and held a small pistol in his hand. He pointed it directly at Margaret's forehead. "I don't think so, do you?"

Chapter Twenty-Two

At the sight of Lord Tumnus, Goldie gave a whimper of fear, pressing close to her sister. Margaret clenched her jaw.

"This has gone too far, *my lord*," she hissed. "You can't possibly intend..."

"My intentions are none of your concern," the man snapped. "They never have been. If you'd minded your own business from the start, none of this would ever have occurred. Now, step aside. Marigold, come here."

"He'll hurt you," Goldie whispered urgently in her sister's ear. "I think he might really shoot. He... he's been acting strangely. I'm more frightened of him than before. He's unpredictable. I don't believe he's ever had to work so hard for something in his life, and it's made him mad. I can't bear to lose you, Margaret."

Margaret swallowed hard, never once tearing her gaze away from Lord Tumnus'. There *was* something odd about his eyes now. They glittered almost maliciously; his face flushed. His hair was dishevelled, and mud lined the hem of his cloak. His hand shook, making the light glint off the short barrel of the pistol, but Margaret did not dare to hope that he would miss. The distance between them was so very small, and there was nowhere for her to go. Nowhere for *Goldie* to go.

Buy time, suggested a small voice in the back of her mind. *Help is coming. It must be.*

Was help coming? Of course, Jasper would be out searching for constables and fetching help. He might not be at home when the carriage driver returned. The driver would wait, of course, allowing more time to tick away. There was no telling whether help *was* coming or not.

Swallowing hard, Margaret met Lord Tumnus' eye squarely.

"Would you really marry a girl who hates you so intensely? How would you live with yourself? How could you sleep at night? Does it not *matter* to you?"

Lord Tumnus smiled grimly, baring his teeth. "Don't talk about what you don't understand, little girl."

"Why not humour me? Make me understand why my mother – my own mother – turned against her daughters."

He shot a quick, contemptuous glance at Lady Keswick, who was standing very still and silent in the shadows.

"Fear of losing what she had, I suppose," he snorted. "Fear of debtor's prison. Fear of humiliation. Your mother, I daresay, has told you that she only played cards to put food on the table and pay the bills. I daresay it all sounded rather noble. Let *me* tell you, my dear, she gambled for another reason entirely. Because she *liked* it. Because it was an addiction for her, like strong liquor or racing horses. She could not give it up, and she's afraid of being found out for her weakness."

Margaret glanced at her mother, whose face was flat and unreadable.

If you'd only told me, Mama. Things could have been quite different, I think. Quite different.

"And what about you, Lord Tumnus?" she said aloud, tearing her gaze away from Lady Keswick to stare at the man pointing a pistol at her. "What are you afraid of, I wonder? What fear keeps *you* up at night?"

He blinked, momentarily taken aback. Then his lip curled, and he bared his teeth again.

"Enough of this," he spat. "You have until the count of three to step aside, and then I will shoot, madam. Marigold, if you wish to spare your sister's life, then come over to me."

Goldie gave another whimper and moved to step forward. But Margaret hung onto her arm, pulling her back and stepping in front of her.

"Margaret, no!"

"Stay behind me, Goldie," Margaret muttered, teeth clenched. "Sir, I have no intention of stepping aside. Therefore, I implore you to end my existence now, or take your leave and be done with it. For I shall not budge an inch."

Lord Tumnus stared at her for a long, taut minute, during which nobody seemed to be breathing, or blinking, or even *existing* at all.

And then, at the end of that minute, Lord Tumnus spoke.

"So be it," he said, voice raspy and gravelly. He tensed his arm, readying the pistol, and Lady Keswick took one reflexive step forward.

"Wait," she gasped, the expression on her shadowy face twisting. "My lord, wait..."

Lord Tumnus was not listening to her. His gaze was fixed on Margaret, his finger curling around the trigger. She breathed in deeply, straightening her spine and steeling herself.

This is it, she thought, swallowing hard. *How strange that it should all end like this.*

And then there was a sound like thunder, growing louder and rapidly approaching. It took Margaret a half-second to understand that she was hearing footsteps.

Lord Tumnus half turned towards the noise, but not quickly enough to save himself. A figure cannoned into him, sending them both tumbling to the ground with a resounding *thud*.

Goldie shrieked, backing away, hands pressed over her mouth. Lady Keswick retreated too, until her back hit the wall, and she stood there as if glued to it.

Margaret, however, stumbled forward, mostly because she had recognized the man almost at once, from his very silhouette.

It was, of course, Jasper.

The two men rolled over and over on the ground. Jasper was younger and doubtless stronger, but Lord Tumnus was larger, and he had a firmer grip on the pistol. He cursed and swore, bucking to try and get Jasper off him. He pointed the pistol directly at Jasper's face, and Margaret heard a strangled cry. She realized with a start that *she* had made that cry and clapped her hand over her mouth.

Jasper grabbed Lord Tumnus' wrist, wrestling the pistol away from his face. He slammed Lord Tumnus' arm down on the ground again and again until the man yelped in pain and released the pistol.

The weapon clattered across the wooden floor, and Margaret dived to snatch it up.

Jasper pulled back, breathing heavily, keeping the older man pinned to the ground.

"The authorities are on their way," he growled. "It's over for you, sir."

Lord Tumnus snarled. "You're just angry you didn't snap up the young one for yourself, aren't you?"

With a graceful motion, Jasper retracted his arm and delivered a firm blow to Lord Tumnus' visage with a sharp, echoing thud. The gentleman recoiled, his body slackening, and his eyes fluttered closed as he succumbed to unconsciousness.

Jasper staggered to his feet, pressing his hand against his ribs.

"He got in a few good blows, I'm afraid," he confessed, turning towards Margaret. "But it's over now. Thankfully, this wretch here," he paused to poke the unconscious Lord Tumnus with the toe of his boot, "left the front door unlocked, and I could run straight in. A magistrate is coming, and I've told him the whole story."

"The carriage driver..."

"Met me on the road, yes. It was a piece of good luck, and I'm glad of it."

He caught Margaret's eye, their gazes tangling for a moment, and she felt as though her breath were caught in her throat. Then he cleared his throat, turning back to Lady Keswick.

"And as for you, *my lady*," he said, voice dangerously low, "you can expect to have your debts called in fully. I shall ensure that you are prosecuted for kidnapping along with this fellow here."

"Have you proof?" Margaret asked, voice shaking.

Jasper nodded. "There was a man in the hallway, two of my footmen have him. It's Lord Tumnus' valet, Hoggins. He's keen to reveal the whole story, which will be helpful to us all. I'm sorry that you'll have to see your mother in irons, Margaret, but there it is."

Lady Keswick took a shaky step forward, face livid. "Not... not gaol, Your Grace. I don't believe I would survive. I... I have made mistakes, but I had my girls' best interests at heart, truly I did!"

"Do you expect us to believe that?" Margaret shot back. She felt on the brink of tears, her voice wobbling again. "How could you, Mama? How *could* you? Do you see what you have done? You've ruined everything. All you had left was us, and neither of us wish to speak up for you. *I* don't want to speak up for you."

There were voices downstairs now, and footsteps thumping across the floorboards. They would come upstairs at any moment, and then it would all be over. Margaret closed her eyes, envisioning the scene – her mother, dragged off to a barred prison cart, the unconscious Lord Tumnus manhandled after her. She imagined the scandal, the spreads on the papers and the snide, nasty little articles in the scandal sheets.

The Stonehaven name would, of course, be dragged into the whole mess. Goldie would not quite be ruined, but there would be consequences, to be sure. She might be seen as *besmirched*, somehow. Of course, if Goldie did not intend to marry, it wasn't too serious, but Margaret desperately wanted her sister to have the opportunity to *choose*.

"I don't want that," Goldie said, her voice high and tense. They all turned to look at her.

She was very pale in the moonlight, the sickly candlelight throwing odd shadows across her face. She was leaning against the newel of the bed as if for support, clutching on with both hands.

"Marigold?" Jasper said gently. "Do you have something to say?"

Goldie bit her lip, closing her eyes. "I don't want my mother to go to prison. I don't want her to go into debtor's prison, either. She... she's wronged me, and I don't know if I'll ever forgive her. I can't imagine ever wanting to see her again, either, but I don't want her to suffer. Does... does that make sense, Margaret? Am I being silly?"

Margaret came to stand beside her sister, drawing her arm through her own.

"No, Goldie, you aren't silly," Margaret said quietly. "You're kind."

She glanced at Jasper, eyebrows raised. He nodded slowly and turned back to Lady Keswick.

"I'll see what I can do," he said heavily. "Lady Keswick, your daughter may have just saved you from a life of imprisonment. It's a pity you couldn't show her the same courtesy. Let me be clear. I will do what I can to prevent you going to prison, and I will take care of your debts..."

Lady Keswick gave a strangled gasp, hands flying to her throat. "You truly mean it, Your Grace? Oh, I..."

Margaret came to stand beside Jasper. "Do not interrupt my husband, Mother."

There was a taut silence after that. Jasper glanced down at Margaret, and she gave a tiny nod. He nodded back, and continued.

"You will sign forms that shall release Marigold to her sister's guardianship. As well as that, you will never try to contact either of your girls again for as long as you live. If they choose to contact you, that's a different matter, but it will be *their* choice, not yours. Do you understand?"

Lady Keswick's face was bone white. She nodded, swallowing thickly.

"I... I agree."

"Good," Jasper turned, holding out a hand to Goldie. "Let's get out of this place, shall we?"

They left Lady Keswick standing in the corner of the bedroom, with the unconscious Lord Tumnus groaning on the floor. Margaret snatched up the candle as she went, plunging them both into darkness.

The three of them made their way down the stairs, past a line of grim-faced men, led by somebody who appeared to be a local magistrate. In the foyer, Margaret saw a man in black livery, sitting miserably between two Stonehaven footmen. He caught her eye and looked away at once, face heavy with guilt.

The valet, then, she thought. *No doubt he was sent to watch our movements. How long has this business been in the planning?*

"My carriage is just outside," Jasper explained. "It's warm and cosy. Goldie, would you mind climbing in and waiting for a moment? I... I'd like to speak to my wife."

The night was cold, the stars peeping out one by one. A fresh breeze stirred Margaret's hair around her face. She breathed in deeply, closing her eyes and tilting back her head.

The carriage creaked as Goldie climbed in, and the door was closed behind her. Margaret opened her eyes, and found Jasper looking at her, his expression intent. An answering spark lit up in her chest.

"I thought," Jasper said carefully, "that this was meant to be a *reconnaissance* mission."

She winced. "I'm sorry, truly I am. But we had no time to waste. Lord Tumnus had gone out to fetch a priest, somebody who'd marry them regardless of what Goldie wanted."

"I'll let the magistrate know to keep an eye out for such a person. I believe Lord Tumnus was the mastermind behind it all. His obsession for your sister had grown dangerous."

She shuddered. "If we'd come only an hour later..."

The sentence was impossible to complete. The words wouldn't come out of her mouth. Abruptly, Jasper stepped closer to her, taking her hands in his.

"But we weren't too late," he said softly. "We arrived on time. We did it, Margaret. Your sister is safe. *You* are safe."

Hesitating only for an instant, Jasper slid his arm around her shoulders, pulling her close. She rested her head against his chest, closing her eyes. Her arms wound around his waist of their own accord, and it occurred to her that she could hear his heart beating under her cheek.

"I could think of nothing else all the way here," Jasper said shakily, his breath brushing the top of her head. "I could only think of you. I was afraid... I was afraid I'd lost you, Margaret. My imagination ran wild, thinking of all the terrible things that might have befallen you. And then when I got into the house, and I heard that valet talk about watching the house, watching *you*, and I saw Lord Tumnus pointing that pistol at you..." he broke off, shuddering. "It was too much for me, Margaret. I haven't been a good husband, I know that, but I... I'll change. I swear it. I'll be better. You *deserve* better."

Margaret pulled back, lifting a tentative hand to cup his cheek.

"You've been a good husband," she assured him. "Ours has been an odd marriage, to be sure, but we can change things, can't we? After all, it's a natural thing for humans to want to improve who they are, isn't it?"

He bit his lip, looking down at her with a tenderness that made Margaret's chest constrict.

"I've come to care for you, Margaret," he said, voice barely louder than a whisper. "More than I could have imagined. More than I *deserved*."

She lifted her other hand, cupping his face. "You deserve everything," she responded hotly. "You deserve to have people see that you're good and kind, *not* simple-minded, not stupid at all. You deserve to be happy, Jasper.

You deserve..." she paused, clearing her throat. "You deserve to have a wife that loves you. And I *do* love you, Jasper."

She heard the breath hitch in his throat.

"You love me?" he whispered, palms warm on her waist. "Do you truly love me, Margaret?"

She giggled, rising up on her tiptoes and pulling down his head so that she could press her forehead against his.

"Yes. Yes, Heaven help me, I love you."

He kissed her then, rough and uncertain, and sparks shot from the crown of her head to the soles of her feet.

"I love you too, Margaret," he responded breathlessly, when they were obliged to break apart to breathe. "I love you so much I can hardly believe there was a time in my life where you were not there."

"Well, there never will be again," she murmured. "I can promise you that."

And then she kissed him again.

Epilogue

One Year Later

Society Left Shocked By Scandalous Elopement!
Dedicated readers of The Chattering Chaperone *will recall that this author mentioned an occasion in which the now-infamous Lady Alice Bow appeared to be trying to win the affections of the young and naive Duke of Brisbourne. A rather desperate act, for a woman of her character and age, but an understandable one.*

This author humbly admits her mistake – if mistake is what it can be called, of course. It seems that Lady Alice Bow was not to be seduced by the young Duke but had another gentlemen in mind altogether.

Lady Alice's fortunes have taken a rather miserable downward turn over the past Season, starting with her rather shocking gossip campaign against the Duchess of Stonehaven. The reclusive Stonehavens, recently returned to Society, have proven to be rather popular, with the young Duchess' Masquerade Ball being dubbed the event of the Season. Lady Alice appeared to be the only person in Society who did not *like the Stonehavens and began to spread some rather poisonous stories about the poor Duchess.*

We shall not bore our readers with an old story. Gossips generally come to no good – a stern warning to this author – and Lady Alice's lies were soon discovered, and she was accordingly shamed. Bereft of friends and with her prospects plummeting, Lady Alice had lately become more desperate than ever to secure a husband.

Perhaps her pursuit of the Duke of Brisbourne met with failure, or perhaps our unfortunate Lady Alice simply made a few missteps. Either way, this author has it on good authority that she has departed her father's home and gone to Scotland with none other than Mr. Henry Havish, known for his charm, good looks, and remarkable amounts of debt.

It is rumoured that Mr. Havish leaves behind several debts of honour, as well as an informal engagement to another young lady with ten thousand pounds a year.

What will become of this mismatch? Ought we to laugh at Lady Alice, or shall we pity her? The Bow family hurries to distance itself from their wayward daughter, but doubtless information will trickle through to The Chattering Chaperone *soon enough. This author will keep her dedicated readers well abreast of any new developments.*

In the meantime, the Season recedes, and another year in Society is over. Almost everybody is leaving London or has left London. However, dear readers, wherever you are going, and with whoever, this author hopes you are happy. Keep your eyes open and your wits about you. Contrary to what the novels claim, life does not end at the altar, with a ring on one's finger. No, it has only just begun. Adventures await, as well as endless amounts of the most thrilling gossip.

God Speed you all to your country-seats – and this author will see you again soon. Sooner than you think, perhaps.

Jasper finished reading, and cleared his throat.

"There," he said, glancing up at Margaret. "How was that? I think that's the smoothest I've ever read anything."

"You did well," she said, smiling. "You're a good reader, Jasper."

"Comparatively speaking," he scoffed, but she saw a tiny smile creep over his face. He folded the paper carefully and set it down on the carriage seat beside him. It was a cold day, and they were bundled up inside the carriage, rugs and furs spread over their legs, and they hurtled through the countryside at a rocketing pace.

"I wish we'd brought something other than *The Chattering Chaperone*, though. I can't stand scandal sheets."

"True," Margaret acknowledged, "But the *Chaperone* is rather flattering to us, isn't it? Only a year in print, and already it's a roaring success. Everybody reads it, and it's always wise to say abreast of what everybody reads. Besides, this one at least is cleverly written, don't you think? Insightful, incisive, but not too cruel."

Jasper pursed his lips, peering down at the sheet. "Sometimes I feel as though there's something familiar about the writing."

Margaret frowned. "What do you mean?"

Jasper sighed, still eyeing the sheet. "Oh, I don't know. Only that there'll be a turn of phrase, or something is said, and it just feels *familiar*. I'm being silly, I suppose. And then I imagine how much time and how clever one must be to notice things like this. And I think of Goldie, with all that writing she does, and yet we never see anything she ever..." he trailed off, worrying his lower lip.

Margaret shifted on the seat, trying to get comfortable. She was in the final month of her pregnancy, and the long carriage journey was not ideal. Still, it had to be done. She'd made up her mind to it.

"I'm not sure I know what you mean, love."

He sighed again, shaking his head. "Nothing, nothing. I'm just tired and fancying odd things. Do you know, Goldie wants to teach me Latin? *Latin.* I can barely manage English."

Margaret chuckled. "She offered me the same. She thinks that because her mind is so sharp and elastic, so is everybody else's. Not that we're dullards, of course, but I certainly wouldn't like to tackle Latin."

"Nor me," Jasper huffed, propping his boots up on the opposite seat. "And what's the name of that ladies' society she's a part of now? They're always reading clever books and talking about clever things. It makes my head ache."

"How should I know?" Margaret laughed. "I'm not part of it. I am proud of my clever little sister, though. It always amuses me when people call her a bluestocking, not realising that she takes it as the highest compliment."

"The ones who make fun of her are the ones who cannot hold a candle to her intellect," Jasper pointed out.

"I couldn't agree more. Are we nearly there, do you think? My back aches from sitting for so long."

Jasper peered out of the window and pulled a face. "Just a few minutes more. We're almost there."

They had reached a little hamlet, with muddy roads and a few curious pedestrians on the road. People shot inquisitive glances at the carriage as it rocked past, then turned around and went on their way.

Margaret's heart was thumping with nerves.

I can't do this, she thought in a rush. *I simply cannot. I shouldn't have come.*

"Margaret?"

She opened her eyes to find Jasper looking at her, concern etched on his face. She smiled faintly.

"Just a little travel-sick, love."

He sighed. "You never get travel sick. Listen, Margaret, we don't have to do this if you do not wish it. We can turn the carriage around and go home at once. I can't bear the thought of you being upset."

She smiled affectionately at him, reaching forward to take his hand. It was a familiar gesture, their fingers locking together as if they were two halves of a whole. As if they were *meant* to be together.

"I want to do this, Jasper. I *must.* You understand, don't you?"

He held her gaze for a long moment, then nodded, slowly. "I'll try to understand. I think I would not have forgiven her, but forgiveness is yours to give."

Margaret let out a long, slow exhale of breath. "Thank you."

The carriage slowed down, climbing a steep, muddy hill. A small house sat on the tip of the hill, windswept and glistening with the recent rain. Silhouetted against the white-grey sky, it seemed taller and larger than it was.

Keswick House had, of course, been sold. A family of Margaret's acquaintance lived there now, when they were in London. So far, she had avoided visiting their home this Season but would likely have to visit next year. By then, though, the place would have been redecorated, and hopefully would not seem like her old home at all.

The carriage rolled to a halt, stopping in the centre of a round, uneven courtyard. Without the rattle of the wheels and the clop of the horses' hooves, silence fell like a heavy, smothering blanket.

They sat there for a moment or two.

"You don't have to get out, you know," Jasper said at last.

Margaret sighed, leaning her head back against the carriage seat and closing her eyes.

"I think I do," she said, after a pause.

So as not to give herself any time to rethink, Margaret climbed out of the carriage at once. Jasper shifted to the entrance, peering down at her.

"Are you sure you don't want me to come in with you?" he asked.

She shook her head. "I'll do this myself. Thank you, though."

"All right. I'll wait here for you."

She smiled affectionately up at him. "Thank you, love."

And then there was nothing for it but to turn away from the carriage and face her mother's home.

With a start, Margaret saw that Lady Keswick was standing at the open door, watching them.

"Hello, Mother," Margaret said. It wasn't Mama anymore. That felt like a childish title, long since given up.

"Hello, Margaret," Lady Keswick responded. "I take it his Grace will stay in the carriage?"

"Yes, we thought it would be better."

Lady Keswick nibbled her lower lip, glancing over Margaret's shoulder at the carriage.

"I thought... well, I thought, perhaps..."

"Goldie isn't here."

Her mother seemed to deflate. "No. No, of course not. Well, come in. I have tea all ready. And some biscuits. Joan, my maid-of-all-work, baked them. She's remarkably talented."

Margaret wordlessly followed her mother inside, glancing around surreptitiously.

This new house, Mulberry Cottage, had been bought with the proceeds of selling Keswick House. It was much smaller, with only one female servant – the aforementioned Joan – and as far as Margaret knew, there was not much society in this quiet little town.

It was quite a step down from the life Lady Keswick had once had. Despite everything that had gone on, Margaret felt a twinge of guilt.

"Mother, you are comfortable here, aren't you? If there are any more…" she paused, searching for the right words, "…*obligations*, then I'm sure that I could…"

"I'm not playing cards anymore, if that is what you mean," Lady Keswick responded, taking Margaret's cloak. The movement revealed Margaret's rounded belly, and she froze, staring down.

"I'm not sure if I mentioned it in my letter," Margaret answered at last, cradling her stomach protectively, "but I'm expecting a child."

Lady Keswick swallowed thickly. "No, you had not mentioned it. But I suppose there is so little communication between us these days, it wouldn't… that is to say, I don't want you to think I'm ungrateful for your letter, or your visit. It's frankly more than I imagine I deserve."

Margaret blinked. "Well. Who are you, and what have you done with my mother?"

Lady Keswick gave a short, timid laugh at this. She shook out Margaret's cloak and hung it up on a peg.

The hallway was small, dark and narrow, and Margaret was relieved to be ushered into a much brighter parlour. As promised, tea-things were laid out on a low table, and a fire burned idly in the hearth.

"I spend most of my time here," Lady Keswick said, ushering Margaret towards the largest and least-threadbare armchair. "It's a pleasant little room. Joan makes a rather nice companion for me, on long winter evenings. I'm fond of her. She doesn't know about…" Lady Keswick faltered, avoiding Margaret's gaze. "She doesn't know I'm here in disgrace."

Margaret bit her lip, looking away. There were a few moments of silence, saved from being awkward by Lady Keswick picking up the teapot and pouring out two cups.

"What made you decide to visit me?" she asked, eyes on the tea. "I was most surprised to receive your letter. I haven't heard from either of you since I moved here. I hadn't expected to, not for a few years at least."

Margaret took a moment to collect her thoughts before responding. She'd known these were the sorts of questions her mother was going to ask. It was entirely natural. And she'd had the entire carriage ride to think of her answers.

And yet, now that the moment came, she couldn't quite get her words together.

"I suppose I've forgiven you," she said at last. "For what you did to me, at least. You were meant to protect us, Mother."

Lady Keswick still had her head bowed.

"I know," she said softly. "I've had a good deal of time to reflect of everything that occurred. Everything that... that I did. I'm to blame for it all. Lord Tumnus may be in gaol, but I feel as though he haunts me. As you know, my aim was always to get you two girls married off, right from when you were children. It's the safest thing for a woman to do in this world. I can see now that I went about it the wrong way." She added the last part frankly, almost unapologetically, and met Margaret's eye. "I can't change it. I wish I could. It's remarkable that you girls are safe and happy despite it."

There was a pause, during which Lady Keswick hesitated and threw an uncertain glance at her daughter.

"Marigold *is* safe and happy, isn't she?"

Margaret nodded. "She's Out, but has no interest in marriage, Not yet, at least. In the future, who knows? She likes to study. You know the sort of thing that interested her – mathematics, geography, science, that sort of thing. Literature, too. There are a number of books she's recommended to me that are quite thrilling."

Lady Keswick allowed herself a small smile. "I'm glad. She always said she wanted to stay with you, even from when she was a child. I used to tell her that you would marry when you were grown up and leave us all behind. I'm glad I was wrong."

There was another silence. Margaret sipped her tea and thought about what to say next.

A gulf had opened up between them, that much was clear. A breach, and only time would tell whether it would be healed or not. A pang shot through her. Wasn't a woman's relationship with her mother meant to be special?

We're guaranteed nothing in life, she reminded herself and set down her teacup.

"I don't know if Goldie will ever forgive you, not properly," Margaret said, meeting her mother's eye. "You did wrong, Mother. You kidnapped her, you tried to force her into marriage... it's like something out of a Mrs. Radcliff novel."

Lady Keswick got abruptly to her feet, crossing the room to stand beside the window. Margaret twisted around to watch her. It was raining again, water coming down the windowpanes. The countryside around was sodden. The driver on top of the carriage, which could be seen from the parlour window, was hunched over and miserable in his caped, waterproof coat.

"I think about my mistakes every day," Lady Keswick murmured. "I have a great list, as long as both my arms put together, as to what I would do differently if I had the chance. But I don't have the chance. I just wish that Marigold knew how sorry I was. Oh, it wouldn't undo anything, I know that. But every day and every night I regret what a fool I was. *Such* a fool."

Margaret closed her eyes.

"Here is what I will do, Mother. I'll go home and ask Goldie if she'd be willing to receive a letter from you. I can't guarantee that she will, and responding will be her business and hers alone. But if she agrees, you can write all of this down. Show her how sorry you are and see what she has to say. Things will never be the same between us, but... well, you might give it a try."

Lady Keswick turned around from the window, face lit up. "Truly? You'd do that for me, Margaret?"

"For Goldie," Margaret said firmly. "I'll promise nothing."

"No, no, of course." Lady Keswick returned to her seat, smiling to herself. "A second chance... no, I won't get ahead of myself. But thank you, Margaret. You... you're a kinder woman than I ever was."

The two women locked eyes, and something like understanding passed between them. Margaret smiled wryly.

"I hope so, Mother. Now. You said something about biscuits?"

***

Half an hour later, Margaret emerged from her mother's house. Lady Keswick saw her to the door, standing in the doorway with her hand shading her eyes against the brightness, as the sun had come out again.

The driver opened the door, helping Margaret into the carriage. The curtains were shut, so her view of Lady Keswick disappeared as soon as the door was closed.

Jasper was curled in the corner of the carriage, patiently waiting for her.

"Well?" he asked, eyebrows raised. "How did it go?"

"Better than I thought," Margaret admitted. "I'll ask Goldie if Mother may write *one* letter to her. I hope she'll agree, but either way, it will be *Goldie's* choice."

Jasper tilted his head to one side. "Do you know, I think you'll make a wonderful mother."

Margaret snorted, leaning back in the seat. "I shall make an *excellent* mother. Whatever hardships and troubles await us with this little one, at least we can be confident about our parenting abilities *now*, eh?"

Jasper chuckled at that, leaning forward to kiss her. Margaret met his lips eagerly, the familiar melting sensation trickling through her. She pulled back, trailing her fingertips across his jaw.

"You're the most beautiful woman in the world, I think," Jasper murmured, his breath tickling her nose.

"Undoubtedly," Margaret said, leaning back with a grin. "I love you beyond words, I'm afraid."

"How unfortunate for you," Jasper remarked drily. "If Goldie chooses to marry, let's hope that she and her chosen love have a better start than *we* did."

She sighed. "I think it would be difficult for them to have a *worse* start."

"You say that, and yet here we are, as happy as can be."

She tilted her head, grinning. "That is an excellent point. Now. Let's use the journey back to practise your reading, shall we? We never finished *The Chattering Chaperone*."

Jasper groaned theatrically, but obediently picked up the paper. Margaret thumped on the roof of the carriage, an instruction for the driver to drive on. They lurched forward.

"Now," Jasper murmured, "Where did we leave off?"

The End

Printed in Great Britain
by Amazon